Beyond The Gates Of Hell

by

Colin Rushton

Other books by this author

Spectator In Hell
Spirit Of The Trenches

Front cover shows Mayer Hersh (top) and (below) his father
Isaac Lajb Hersckowicz who died in the gas chambers at
Auschwitz during August 1944.

Beyond The Gates Of Hell

by

Colin Rushton

Publisher
Mediaworld PR Ltd
Best Books Online

ISBN: 1-904502-46-6

Chapter One

Over the last three years Mayer Hersh had become a good friend of mine. A survivor of the Holocaust, this serene and quietly spoken man had always sought to close down any enquiring sorties into that emotive subject. "It was a long time ago", was one of his more common closures.

In recent weeks I had noticed his sublime serenity had become seriously disturbed and I queried to myself the reason for this change in a quality that was essentially what he was all about. I was not to wait long for the solution to the puzzle. It was Tuesday April 9th 2002 as I awaited an answer to my ringing his doorbell. To my surprise, his wife, Judith, opened the front door. "He's gone to Auschwitz, left at 3am and won't be back till near midnight," was her surprising retort to my questioning his whereabouts. Judith went on to point out that she had genuinely tried to persuade him not to make the trip for fear of acutely distressing himself.

Mayer, however, had apparently begun to have thoughts of telling his story so that younger generations could be educated in exactly what happened in Europe at the hands of the Third Reich, no doubt influenced by some of the party of Manchester Jews with whom he had travelled.

Sensing the possible unfolding of a spectacularly moving account, I determined to contact Mayer two days later. On our first meeting I was surprised to find his serenity had returned in full and he was keen to talk. I immediately came to the conclusion that re-visiting Auschwitz had been an undoubted success and an experience he was so pleased he'd undertaken. "I had sworn never to see Auschwitz again for, in the fall of 1987, my best friend, David Josefowicz, and myself visited Chelmno." The strongest emotion crackled in his voice and he took a minute or two to compose himself. "Four hundred thousand Jews from Western Poland were killed and cremated there, my mother and three younger brothers amongst them. David and I were totally emotionally destroyed, and from that moment on, Auschwitz was never in our itinerary."

Asking whether I could tape the proceedings, Mayer nodded approvingly and I went on to state that he should tell his story for posterity and possibly help to prevent a repeat of those darkest of deeds in the history of man. "What better than a book, capable of doing that job even long after you've left this world," I countered. Mayer smiled his agreement and two friends had a pact.

For Mayer the return to Polish Silesia was akin to stirring a clear pool with a stick and disturbing the underlying soil, his mind was muddied with swirling emotions and memories. Two hundred and thirty five flew from Manchester to Krakow on Yom Hashoah, Holocaust Day in the Hebrew calendar, Tuesday April 9th 2002. Amongst this number were some non Jews and, after much pleading from numerous colleagues, Mayer agreed to return nearly fifty eight years after last setting eyes on the belching crematoria chimneys. He was the only survivor in the Manchester party and, after a two-hour flight and a one-hour road journey, in just three hours he was back at the gates of hell.

2

The 'March of the Living' from Auschwitz to Birkenau takes place annually and is a protest, an affirmation, that despite Nazi attempts to eliminate all European Jewry, some have survived. With other groups coming from France, Germany, North America and Israel, the latter group being by far the largest, they walked slowly with dignity, without hatred, and with pride.

Whilst making a post war return with his friend David Josefowicz to Chelmno, the two survivors broke down completely with acute mental anguish, so badly in fact that visiting Auschwitz was considered totally out of the question on that occasion and at any time in the future. Chelmno was the God forsaken place where nearly all of their relatives, schoolmates and indeed most of their hometown community perished, innocent people humiliated, prior to being murdered.

What then made him change his mind this time? "You've got to do it for the younger generations, you have got to give them the hope, the courage that Jewish people have survived and can do so in the future." That was the impassioned plea that finally persuaded him to make the trip to the ultimate destination of torment and brutality, utterly and totally devoid of any hope for the future.

He was so pleased he went, for the concern and sensitivity shown to him by the fifteen year olds on the visit moved him to tears. They were constantly watching Mayer, with sadness in their eyes, their sincerity expressed. They were so calm and dignified that he felt both great and humble sharing the moment with them. The youngsters clearly found it incomprehensible to understand how human beings could sink to such depths of total barbarity and depravity.

The media were much in evidence with BBC Television,

Manchester Evening News and Granada Television accompanying the party. This was not surprising really, for Auschwitz was, and always will be, very special, its dark deeds putting it into a classification of its own. It was here that young Mayer, then sixteen years of age, realised the vast scale of the Holocaust, for every nationality passed through its gates. Prisoners unable to comprehend the German language, and there were many in this category, were dead meat with no hope of survival, for there were no second commands given.

A few in the line were in wheelchairs and Mayer went over to one of these unfortunates, an unashamed lump in his throat, "I feel honoured to see a man in your physical state giving a smack in the eye to Nazism. If Hitler was alive today and could see some survivors of his camps, being accompanied by Jewish youth, and marching in Auschwitz with abundant sandwiches in their pockets, he would no doubt commit suicide.

The long line left Auschwitz and, at a slow walk, covered the approximately four kilometres to reach Birkenau, an extermination camp like none other, where millions were gassed and yet not one gravestone could be seen. This place had been Mayer's home for eighteen long months and the arrival there was to be his most painful moment. Prayers were said for all the innocent souls who had been converted to ash, which was liberally tipped in the nearby River Ner. This service took place at a monument near one of the crematoria and finished with an Israeli singing a prayer entitled 'I Believe', as beautiful as it was moving. He found what was left of his barrack D24, hut 24 in D camp, merely the concrete base with a fireplace and a chimney at each end. As he stood on the floor he had cleaned on numerous

4

occasions, memories of single incidents flooded back and these constituted his most emotional moments. The fireplaces before the war had been lit in order to keep the horses warm but no such luxuries were afforded to the Jews. The multitude of cracks in the wooden walls through which the coldest of Polish winter winds would whistle, could not be seen, for all wood was commandeered after hostilities had ceased, for barns and stables. The end of D Camp was opposite the main railway ramp and the inmates of D24 had good views of the never-ending hordes of arrivals from all parts of Europe.

The gap between D24 and the next barrack was the site where all occupants of D24 were put through that obnoxious operation, roll call, twice a day, morning and evening. For inmates there accrued a multitude of painful memories with many sessions lasting hours in often extreme climatic conditions, this being yet another torment exercised by their Nazi hosts. There were two latrines in D Camp, each occupying the same area as a barrack holding one thousand men. Mayer's camp was maybe only two hundred yards, at its closest point, to the nearest crematorium, all four dispatchers of evidence being cleverly disguised by poplar trees in an attempt to allay the fears of the new arrivals. Nevertheless only a blind man would fail to see the flames and smoke belching forth from their tall chimneys, but that stench of burning flesh would fool nobody. The watchtowers and the barbed wire fences, on which so many, who could take no more torment, electrocuted themselves, these were the sights that hit Mayer hard. Next to D Camp was the gypsy camp, E Camp, the visit revealing to Mayer something he never knew previously, that in fact Jews were also held prisoner in E Camp, all occupants of which were totally eliminated on one April day in 1944. Crossing over the railway track he visited a barrack in the women's camp and was amazed at what he saw. Half the barrack was for occupation by the prisoners and the other half was a latrine. The building was complete with the exception of the total absence of the timber bunk beds but, on leaving, his mind could not come to terms with trying to imagine the intolerable stench from that indoor latrine.

During his fifty-six years spent in the United Kingdom he had always been inwardly aware of the importance of survivors telling ensuing generations about the horrific Nazi persecution of the Jews during World War Two. He recognised that knowledge of what had happened was the key to preventing a repeat of the inhuman disasters but, being a very private person, he had never gone out to seek opportunities to fulfil his feelings. This was it, this was his acid test, his chance to tell the world of younger generations exactly how it was to have your schooling rudely terminated at the tender age of twelve. How it was to be dragged from the bosom of a close and loving family and, with one exception, never to see any of his immediate kin ever again. To be beaten and starved, and generally, to suffer the prejudiced wrath of numerous races simply because he was a Jew, albeit totally innocent of any crime.

He was nervously fidgeting with his first United Kingdom passport as he prepared to start the tale of his marathon of miseries that would eventually stretch over more than fifteen hundred miles of cattle truck transport, covering five years two months of hard labour in no less than nine camps. Mayer Hersh explained how precious that first British document was, for it identified his family name, his biological birthright. Every subsequent passport had simply read 'Mayer Hersh' where that initial 1955 copy declared 'Mayer Hersh originally known as Herszkowicz'.

Mayer's family came from the town of Sieradz in pre-war Western Poland, only 75 kilometres from the then German border. They lived in a one bed-roomed flat on the second floor of a building in the oldest part of town, built around 1818, at number seven Ulica Sukiennicza, an address Mayer shared with his parents, sister and four brothers. In English the street name translates to Dressmaker Street, a leaning to distant times when certain trades concentrated in specific areas. Although economically times were exceedingly difficult, this very close knit, loving family enjoyed many very happy and contented times together, notwithstanding the ever-deepening shadows of anti-Semitism, rife in Poland, especially during the latter half of the thirties. Both Mayer and his father experienced exceedingly distasteful incidents of racial hatred at this time.

Chapter Two

Over the centuries Jews have always been a persecuted race, but when considering anti-Semitism existing in Poland during the thirties, one needs to appreciate the political background in that country. The Catholic church was at the forefront of this racial hatred, both before and during this decade, ably assisted by the aristocracy. It showed itself as hostile graffiti on public walls and pavements, a typical message declaring, 'go back to Palestine you dirty Jews'. Marshal Pilsudski was Prime Minister as the nineteen thirties opened their doors, presiding over the thirty five million Polish population, ten percent of which were Jews. He was not anti-Semitic and, being a very fair minded man, considered Jews born in or even merely living in Poland, as Poles. In the face of this racial animosity he had the foresight to believe that the great skills in trades and commerce that the Jews possessed would help build a better Poland. Unfortunately in 1935 this most popular and charismatic man passed peacefully away and Mayer missed one day's education as the whole school was taken to the cinema to see the funeral and national mourning of the people's hero. His position was filled by Szmygly Rydz, not as fair a man as his predecessor, so consequently the graffiti increased and many Jews, including Mayer himself, experienced violent verbal and physical attacks. The Jewish nation has always wandered the Earth and national borders were more open in those days than they are today, so consequently to cross from one country to another they need only be able to afford to reach the border. The Jews were always grateful for being allowed to live in that country and earn a living, thereby keeping their heads down and not looking for trouble. This passive attitude signalled to the world a reluctance to fight back. Throughout history they have been blamed for spreading epidemics and yet all they've ever wanted was peace and to be allowed to work. When the Holocaust came the Jews were not ready to fight.

Mayer went on to explain that the clouds of war had been gathering and ordinary people, Jews included, honestly believed war would take place, but there was no panic, for these people had experienced the first World War, when the German occupying forces showed exemplary behaviour and business with them was excellent. There was no way any of them could have foreseen the levels of brutality that went under the name, Holocaust. Nevertheless some of the more affluent Jews did leave the European mainland in the early part of 1939, travelling to countries like the Americas, both north and south, Britain and Israel, just in case the worst might happen. Later the borders to France and Holland were closed.

A neutral observer could have been excused for assuming that the more affluent Jews were more informed generally because there had been warnings, one as early as 1895 in Hermann Ahlwardt's speech to the Reichstag. *'The Jew is no German. If you say that a Jew is born in Germany, has obeyed German laws, has had to become a soldier, has fulfilled all his duties, has paid his taxes too, then all that is not decisive for nationality, but only the race out of which he was born is decisive.*

'In 1933 Josef Goebbels coldly announced, *'As to*

annihilate German Jewry, let no one doubt our resolution.'
Three years later the same high-ranking official declared, *'A time of brutality approaches of which we have no conception.'*

On the third of March 1933 Hermann Goering stated, *'My measures will not be hindered by any legal considerations or bureaucracy whatsoever. It is not justice I have to carry out, but annihilation and extermination.'* On the twelfth of November 1938, the same Nazi showman had this to say, *'Kick out the Jews from the economy and turn them into debtors.'*

On July 5th 1938 the Western powers held the Evian conference in France where they did nothing in relation to the more and more threatening situations for Jews in Europe. Apparently it has come to light in recent years that the British government decreed that it would only attend this conference on condition that Palestine was not to be on the agenda. The following words were spoken by Adolf Hitler on January 20th 1939 as a direct reply to the lack of action from the Western powers. *'It is a shameless spectacle to see how the whole democratic world is oozing sympathy for the poor tormented Jewish people, but remains hardhearted and obdurate when it comes to helping them.'* The non committal attitude of the free world is best epitomised by considering the remark made by the Australian delegate, *'since we have no racial problem, we are not desirous of importing one.'* In a voice laden with sadness and emotion Mayer continued, mentioning that there is a saying which is most appropriate in this instance: "all that is needed for evil to triumph is for good people to do nothing".

Finally when action against the Jews was well underway,

the following statement came from the mouth of Josef Goebbels on the sixteenth of November 1941. *'By reason of their birth and race, all Jews are part of an international conspiracy against National Socialist Germany. The treatment we give them does them no wrong. They have more than deserved it.'*

Probably unbeknown to most ordinary folk, Nazism had, at its roots, the belief that Jews were evil parasites and sexual predators, grasping capitalists as well as Marxist conspirators. This perverted philosophy blamed the Jews of Europe and America for the First World War, the Great Depression and the spread of Bolshevism. This vile doctrine looked upon the Jewish race as one of lower standing, needing less room, less clothing, less food and less culture than a race of higher standing. Given all these distorted beliefs, and in hindsight, it was in all probability not surprising that the leaders of this dark age, with meticulous attention to detail, gave birth to the greatest monster of the twentieth century, 'die Endlosung', the final solution.

Sieradz had a total population of 12,000, of which 5,000 were Jews, a similar number of Catholic Poles and the remainder ethnic Germans. There was anti-Semitism in Poland before, during and after the war. Before the war the main culprits would be the Catholic Poles, whilst once the Germans had invaded and taken occupation, the ethnic Germans would be mostly the collaborators with the Third Reich. The main Schul, or synagogue, in Sieradz could hold a thousand Jews at worship, whilst the second in size for religious meetings was the Beit Hamidrash, a religious place of learning and for prayer. In addition there were numerous stiebels in the town, the word in German meaning room, which were not large, but served as prayer rooms.

Mayer's father, Isaac Lajb Herszkowicz, born in 1896 in Lask 33 kms away from Sieradz, had had a very religious upbringing and could speak Polish, German, Russian and Yiddish.

His mother, Riwka Rachel Szczukowska, was born in Kalisz, near Poznan, and approximately 50 kms from Sieradz. Kalisz was then in Germany until 1918 when it became part of Poland. She received Hebrew, German and Polish education and, although orphaned and losing her home due to the first World War, never felt bitter about that fact.

Isaac Herszkowicz had married previously but his first wife had died at the tender age of 22 years, leaving him with two babies, Yakov and Kajla. He was a happy being normally, often singing, but nevertheless was afraid of no man. He did, however, usually conform with his own mother's advice and, when she recommended a cousin of his first wife's as being of good stock, he married the lady who was to become Mayer's mother. Mayer himself was a shy lad, not particularly sports minded and somewhat withdrawn, being, metaphorically speaking, diametrically opposite to his elder brother, Yakov, who was a very outgoing person, always with a good crowd of friends and very much into sports. He played football in bare feet because their father could not afford football boots, the lack of affluence of the Herszkowicz family earning them the description of 'quite poor'. Many Jews were significantly poorer, and some children went to bed half starved, waking up in the middle of the night from pangs of hunger, crying for a piece of dry bread. Yakov was a strong physical boy who helped his father with heavy fetching and carrying and also had keen sight to prevent pilfering by many Christians, a state of affairs polarised by the stark poverty present at that time. It is often stated by non Jews that there are never any poor Jews, but that was certainly not the case in Sieradz in 1939.

Although a well-to-do Jew owned the flourmill in the town, most of them were experiencing hard times pre war, due, in no small part, to the restrictive legislation imposed on Jews over the centuries. Jewish people were thus forced to choose from the very narrow band of trades that were accessible to them, namely, tailoring, saddlery, glazing, shoemaking, joinery, shopkeepers, barbers and bakers. Too many people doing the same job led to too competitive a price to survive. His father was a tailor and a good one, who served his apprenticeship at Brzezin near Lodz. He was a canny man, for he would make cheaper suits, where his money was much safer, rather than their expensive counterparts, which would often lead to ruin for the manufacturer. He worked from home on the family's one and only table and, being an excellent manager and working on wafer thin margins, his keen prices put others out of business and he would often buy their stock at a discounted price. He made up stock for home and market and he worked so quickly that he could make thirty pairs of trousers per day on a treadle machine. He counted numerous farmers on his customer list and they would often come for funeral clothes, which were a most lucrative line due to people being superstitious and so would not bargain down. Most of his customers were non Jews and he would always ask after the family, or their livestock, impressing them all with his excellent customer relationships. Nevertheless he did have his competition, for there was also a tailor below on the

13

first floor who was not above virtually dragging customers in off the stairs in pursuit of sales. Mayer's father took his daughter, Kajla, out from school early for she was an excellent worker with a keen brain and, with her help, the business prospered.

Mayer's mother was not particularly interested in business matters, partly due to the fact that she had to bring up seven children when she married his father who, as a widower, already had two children from his first marriage. His mother lost her first child when less than two years old but nevertheless continued to be the rock on which their happy family life was built. She cooked and cooked with love and was always extremely busy, so much so that he remembers asking her why she didn't ask the children to help her. She would buy chickens and take them to the slaughterhouse, for koshering the meat, by thoroughly draining all blood, was a meticulous job. For Passover his mother would buy many eggs and potatoes, storing the eggs in numerous drawers. She would manage the space and services of their one room flat, a space about 16 feet square, for the eating and sleeping habits of eight people and the self employed requirements of one tailor. Their attic room on the top floor of the building made the worst of Poland's widely varied climate. The unbearable heat of summer making sleep virtually impossible, whilst the extreme winter temperatures would freeze a bucket of water. There were two permanent and three collapsible beds and privacy for the parents was obviously at a premium. On Thursday mornings mother, with any of her children not in school, would take cake and chala, plaited bread for the Sabbath, to the bakers, from where they would collect the cooked product on Friday for Shabat. Also on Friday the children would take cholen, a big pot made up of chicken or other meats with potatoes and butter beans, or Kasza, a type of barley. This was collected about noon, after prayers, from the baker. It was a most delicious meal, the word 'cholen' believed to be derived from the French phrase 'chaud long', meaning staying hot.

Mayer attended the Powszechny mixed comprehensive school where he studied Mathematics, English, Geography, History and Music from a variety of good and indifferent teachers. One teacher stood out in his memory for the wrong reasons, his lady maths teacher, Najmanowa, born a Jew but who since had turned to Christianity. He had been off ill for two weeks and, on his return, the teacher asked him questions he was unable to answer because of missing the work. "That's your problem," was her abrupt reply, for which Mayer disliked her and could never forget or forgive her lack of human feeling. When a pupil met a teacher in the street he had to doff his cap but, when war broke out and the ghetto was formed in the Herszkowicz's part of the town, her conversion to Christianity cut no ice with the Germans for, in their eyes, born a Jew meant always a Jew. She was transferred to Mayer's building and it brought him great pleasure not lifting his cap to her again. Although a Jewish school, the staff were mixed and one of his favourite members of staff was Weichmanowa, a lovely ethnic German lady and an excellent history teacher but one who suffered somewhat for her inability to maintain discipline.

Mayer also followed his Hebrew education by attending the Cheder school where discipline was strict. One tall male teacher, nicknamed 'Stoik', made liberal use of a cat o' nine tails with the full permission of all the fathers of the pupils. This man also doubled as a doctor, although not a physician in the true sense of the word, he was well respected in his secondary profession and once tended Mayer with tonsilitis, issuing a prescription to cover necessary treatment. One day Mayer addressed him by his nickname and the teacher chased the boy home with his cat o' nine tails, the pupil hiding up in the house until passions cooled somewhat.

Mayer did not have any great ambitions but, since he showed some academic ability, his father promised him higher education, secular as well as Hebrew. To this end he sent him to another Hebrew teacher and paid for the privilege. This man was an excellent teacher in Jewish history and taught even on Shabat afternoon in classes of between ten and fifteen. Even without this extra paid education, school was a six-day week, Shabat excepted, with primary school starting at seven years of age and running from 8am to 1pm. Hebrew school started for pupils of five years and lasted for three hours in the afternoons.

Mayer's very best friend was David Josefowicz, whose mother had died pre war in the thirties, and who lived in Castle Street with his father, Henoch, and his brothers and sisters. They had what currently one would describe as a terraced town house which was much more upmarket than the Herszkowicz's flat in Dressmaker Street. David's dad bought livestock from farmers, usually chickens and geese, which were kept in their own backyard, a precious possession denied many of the poorer people. Henoch was an entrepreneur, a taker of risks, and it was soon to become apparent, during the occupation, that David shared that same quality with his father. With the acumen of a specialist, his father would buy off whole orchards of green fruit on the edge of town. He would then be responsible for the successful growing on of the fruit, including watering, spraying and marketing. There was always an element of risk in fruit growing, some years doing very well, others not so well. In July during the school holidays Mayer and David passed many happy days picking fruit, usually soft fruit like gooseberries, bilberries and cherries. Both the young lads enjoying the companionship, not to mention the fruit!

Mayer remembered those pre war days as being basically happy but marred by the anti-Semitism endemic at that time. His father, a good man who more than once helped a poor neighbour with money for food for their hungry children, and yet was verbally abused and physically attacked just because he was a Jew. Likewise Mayer himself endured this evil malice when a boy pushed a piece of non koshered sausage into his mouth and another lad kept continually taunting him with the despicable phrase, 'you dirty Jew'. Now Mayer was, and still is, the most mild mannered of men and one of the last to lose his composure, but eventually that name caused him to snap and drop a brick on the youth's head. The latter never called him a dirty Jew ever again.

Jews were restricted to certain trades and, in order that this restriction be maintained in the future, as far as possible, only ten percent maximum of Jewish applicants for higher education were to be granted such a privilege. This percentage figure was arrived at due to the Jewish population being ten percent of the full Polish population. Consequently if in any one year, one hundred Jews applied for higher education, only ten would be given the opportunity of advancement in their chosen career, be it doctor, vet or lawyer. Having said anti-Semitism existed extensively in the thirties, Jews got by because non Jews always wanted their best deal and these more privileged citizens knew that a more attractive price was always to be had from a Jew, their skills in trading and business in general already being legendary.

He remembered a number of the neighbours in those days when events in Germany were casting an ever-lengthening shadow over the rest of Europe. There was a very religious Jewish family on the ground floor who ran a haberdashery stall in the market on Tuesdays and Fridays. The wife of the family would deliver children in the neighbourhood and actually officiated in the births of his three younger brothers.

Mayer could picture in his mind Mordechai der wassertreger, the water carrier, who also lived on the second floor, as an old man, although probably only in his forties. He would deliver water to people who could afford to pay, in two wooden buckets attached to a yoke around his shoulders. There was another water carrier in the town, a more up market version, whose horse drawn tanker was quite an advanced improvement for a small town like Sieradz, both collected their product via the pumps in either Market Square or Castle Street. Mordechai was a poor man who, out of necessity, existed on bread and kasza (barley). In winter when the temperature dropped to very low levels one, or even both, pumps would actually freeze up, causing significant inconvenience, not to mention putting two hard workers out of a job.

The caretaker of the block of flats was the only non Jew, Kazimierz Kruk, a heavy drinker who would beat his wonderful wife with a knotted towel or belt. He could not keep money and Mayer's father and others helped them manage their finances. Kruk visited Germany and he returned overwhelmed with the medical benefit system they enjoyed and was most impressed with how well off the German people were with their high standard of living. He enjoyed making a dramatic statement in the courtyard to a group of anxious Jews, Mayer could still hear his words, 'when the Germans come in, they'll cut off all Jewish heads.' Sadly his prophecy came true. That the Germans would invade there was little doubt, this state of affairs being enhanced when 15,000 Polish born Jews, who had lived in the Fatherland for ten, twenty and even thirty years, were given notice of eviction. He remembered early in October 1938 when the Polish government stated that all Jews who had lived outside Poland for more than five years would have their passports revoked. The Germans immediately announced there would no longer be a place inside their country for these 'stateless' people. On October 18th 1938 these hapless and helpless people were forced to leave their homes with just one suitcase per person and escorted to the nearest railway station, leaving the rest of their belongings behind. They were transported through the night to the German/Polish border and forced over at gunpoint.

Sonheim was the landlord who lived with his family on the ground floor in more spacious accommodation with his own toilet but, like the tenants, had no running water. His married children and extended family would occupy separate flats within the block of flats. The property owners were very good hearted and compassionate people. If some of the tenants had difficulties with the rent payment they would always show understanding. Since nobody in those days possessed a fridge, the landlord would allow Mayer's family to use his cellar for some of their cooked food. Using an oil press in the basement, Sonheim also made money on oil from rapeseed and on residual cake to farmers for cattle feed as well as revenue from his granary situated in his backyard. One night the German soldiers raided a few homes including the Sonheim family. All these people were so chosen because they were influential and respectable in the local community and, materially, better off than most. These deportations the Germans euphemistically described as aussiedlung, meaning resettlement. The victims were either murdered on arrival or died in the gassing vans, to be cremated at Chelmno.

Most Jews in Sieradz were orthodox with a small minority of liberal persuasion, these being mainly ethnic German Jews, who had their own Schul and lived in the better part of town.

Mayer respected his father greatly and could picture him beavering away in his very ordinary suit and a cap and always sporting a short beard. During the week he was usually quite tense but Friday and Saturday saw him more relaxed and happy. He was a courageous man and afraid of nobody. Yiddish was spoken in family circles whilst outside and in school Polish was used.

Another person who was a familiar caller to the Herszkowicz household in the late thirties was Arnold Kupfer, a young man in his twenties born in Germany and whose father was a Polish Jew. He was going out with Mayer's sister, Kajla, and reasonably soon the two became engaged. Both wanted to emigrate to Palestine, for Arnold was of the opinion that the future for Jews in Europe was black indeed, but they encountered strong resistance from Kajla's father, not wanting to lose his daughter for she was such an asset to his business. As early as 1936/37 Mayer's sister and elder brother, Yakov, wanted to emigrate to Palestine but unfortunately the British Mandatory Authority would not give permission. In March 1939 Arnold managed to obtain emigration papers for Uruguay but her father continued to insist that she could not go. Arnold wrote often to Kajla from South America but by then it was too late for his fiancée, trapped by the war. Years later, Arnold eventually reached his goal, Israel.

Immediately before war was declared Mayer witnessed a horrible example of anti- Semitic behaviour that cast a shadow over Sieradz like a black cloud before a storm. A young Catholic priest, an educated man, went to the market and told customers not to buy from Jews. In minutes the market place was deserted, for most of the customers were non Jews and to them the word of a priest was to be obeyed in preference to that of the police. This man of God, who preached to his congregation to love thy neighbour, had lost his way with respect to his calling and it served as an ominous warning to Jews of the dark days ahead that they were about to endure. In those tension charged weeks in late August 1939 Jews were stung visibly by anti-Semitic slurs, especially from a man of the cloth. The following market day, however, the non Jews wanted their best prices once again, and all the customers returned.

Chapter Three

The memories of his thirteenth birthday on Thursday 31st August 1939 flooded back into his mind vividly as if it were yesterday. This was to be the last day of peace that his native Poland was to enjoy for some considerable time. "You won't be starting your school term today, Mayer", he could still hear his father's words ringing in his ears. "The German forces have invaded". It was 6.30 am on Friday 1st September as his dad stood at the foot of his bed. Even the absence of both radio and newspapers could not prevent such news spreading like wildfire in his home community of Sieradz, near Lodz, in pre-war western Poland. Unbeknown to young Mayer his school would never re-open ever again and his formal education had ended at the tender age of twelve.

Initially young Mayer was quite excited, a real war in his mind meant exciting adventures with plenty of action. In reality they were the saddest years of his life and it wasn't long before the smile was wiped off his face when he became aware just how worried his mother and father were. With Sieradz being most important strategically, his mother asked him to walk to his uncle's house in Zdunska Wola, fourteen kilometres distant in a due east direction, to ask if they could stay there until the fighting ceased. He returned the same day with an affirmative answer from his uncle, a weaver by trade, and, with his father hiring a cart and two horses, they began making their way with some neighbours on the Saturday to Zdunska Wola, a town famous for weaving cotton. As they left to cross the brand new bridge over the River Warta they came across Mayer's cousin, Avrom Najman, in the uniform of the Polish army, only to be told that he was awaiting instructions to blow the bridge up. Mayer remembered thinking at the time of the tragically wasteful loss of the new construction, a valuable asset squandered in the cause of warfare. They said their farewells and moved on, never to see Avrom again for he was to perish, like so many others, at Auschwitz.

Sheltering with numerous others in his uncle's garden, the starkest fear gripped everyone as German planes dived low, using anything and everything for target practice. Some of their neighbours were injured and even killed in those initial aerial strikes, which continued through Saturday and Sunday. On the Monday morning a deathly silence had transcended the scene when Mayer and a friend plucked up courage to venture out onto the main road. Nothing was moving, an eerie silence accompanying the many dead bodies and horses blown to pieces. Suddenly a German scout car came racing around the bend with machine guns mounted on both sides and the two boys realised that German troops would be occupying the town in minutes rather than hours.

He was absolutely amazed at the enormous number of huge swastika flags that suddenly hung from every flag pole and most top floor windows the moment the Germans entered Zdunska Wola on that Sunday the 3rd September 1939. The transformation was eye-catching and sinister at the same time, for the aggressors received a very warm welcome from the volksdeutsche. There were about ten thousand Jews and possibly a few more ethnic Germans, the balance being Poles making up the twenty five thousand population of this town, which was considerably larger than Sieradz. The ethnic Germans must have been preparing those multitudes of swastikas for some considerable time and their anti-Semitic views were to harden considerably in the weeks to come. The sudden preponderance of fluttering swastikas served as an ominous foreboding of an uncertain future. Suddenly the safety of the Great War occupation seemed far less relevant to Jews.

Once the occupation had settled down the family decided to return to Sieradz, providing their house was still standing. This fact was confirmed in the affirmative by Mayer, and his elder brother Yakov, again on foot, checking and reporting back. Within days of their returning home the Germans destroyed their synagogue, completely vandalised it and burnt all the holy books. In no time at all this sacred place was turned into a skeleton of its former self and eventually became a hay barn. Other religious buildings were similarly treated and Jews were not allowed ever to meet for religious prayer on pain of death. Rabbis and other church leaders were singled out and killed immediately but, in one instance, in the small community of Warta, fifteen kilometres from Sieradz, the Germans obtained maximum pleasure and enjoyment by insisting a son hanged his own Rabbi father. The boy instinctively went to refuse but his father nodded his approval for he knew the Nazis would kill him anyway and while his son lived there was always hope for him. Immediately after he had executed his father however, the son was shot by the Nazis. This all took place before a good sized crowd, the Germans saw to that, thereby adding the pain of humiliation and shame to that of death for the young man. The Germans were to excel at public degradation.

Apparently when the Germans first tried to capture Sieradz there was fierce hand to hand fighting at which the Poles excel and the Germans were forced to retreat. The invaders then resorted to heavy artillery to soften the place up before they took Sieradz with superior numbers but only as late as the 20th September 1939.

During the fighting when the Germans entered the town, a Catholic priest, Chaplin to the Polish forces, was attending to a wounded Polish soldier in the streets of Sieradz. He was immediately arrested and sent to one of the concentration camps although he, fortunately, managed to survive the camps and the war. Virtually immediately atrocities commenced and male Jews had their beards burnt off their faces. The civilian population thought and hoped that brutalities would be limited, remembering clearly the Germans' exemplary behaviour during World War One occupation, but the inhumane treatment of the Jews escalated both in scale and regularity. Sieradz and the surrounding areas were immediately annexed to the Third Reich, who renamed the composite area, Warthegau. This newly named region ran north as far as the River Warte, which approximated to one hundred kilometres. In the first six weeks of occupation, no less than 16,336 Polish civilians were executed in 714 localities, of which at least 5,000 were Jews. Life was never to be the same again.

These deaths came after those incurred by the Polish army, who fought with skill and bravery at many battles, checking German progress time and again before eventually relenting to superior manpower and armaments. During the fighting, more than sixty thousand Polish soldiers were killed, of whom some six thousand were Jews. The race that was the butt of the intense anti-Semitic propaganda was about to enter the darkest days of its existence in Poland, for Jews had been a part of that country from as early as the tenth century in the township known as Luck, the latest arrivals coming in the nineteenth century to Sosnowiec.

One comparatively well-to-do family who also had clearly decided that Poland under the Nazis was not the place to be, was the Bulka family, who owned the flour mill in the town. Mayer knew their son, Zamek, and he and the whole family escaped to Russia and survived the war. They crossed while the German/Russian border was still open, this latter frontier closing on the 31st November 1939. In effect on 28th September 1939 Poland was partitioned between Nazi Germany and the Soviet Union. In that two month period more than a quarter of a million Jews escaped from the German to the Russian side and these people were to constitute the majority of the survivors of Polish Jewry at the termination of hostilities.

Shortly afterwards Mayer was due his bar mitzvah, as a thirteen year old, for his day of confirmation. This happy occasion, looked forward to longingly by all members of his family, he was never allowed to enjoy. Losing this extra special function constituted a major disappointment and loss in his young life and, although there is no rule declaring a Jew has to conform to this ceremony, it is customary to have a second bar mitzvah at the age of eighty three years, three score years and ten beyond the thirteenth birthday.

Mayer was soon to witness the darker side of life in occupation. One evening a German soldier was walking along close to the family home when suddenly he shot his rifle into the air, claiming he had been shot at by one of the Jews. Later that same night some of Mayer's neighbours were dragged out of their beds in the early hours only to be lined up against a wall and shot, despite their pleadings for mercy. The Herszkowicz family heard the Germans running up the stairs to the first floor, screaming obscenities and physically forcing Jewish families out onto the street below. Those innocent people, their chilling screams piercing the darkness, were dragged from their beds so unceremoniously, lined up and their lives terminated as though it was an exercise for the troops. Fortunately for Mayer and his family, the enemy did not try the second floor. The absolute fear his parents were showing at this time, thinking they would be next, was a sight he can never forget. The bloodstained wall, dramatically portrayed the following morning in daylight, made everyone wonder what the future held for them all. These ruthless Nazi atrocities on Dressmaker Street rendered every Jewish heart heavy with fear yet, barbaric as they most certainly were, the split second snapshot that has remained in his mind to this day was the absolute fear in his parents' eyes as the Germans clattered their way up the stairs toward flat number seven. Words could not describe that look, suffice to say its powerful image made a tremendous impression on thirteen year old Mayer, penetrating through his mind and making him much more fearful of what the future held in store.

On another occasion all the men of the town were forced to assemble in the main square and kept there indefinitely. All the time never knowing whether they would ever see their families again. Late that night some of these men were lined up and marched off, never to be seen again. The remainder of the men returned to their families, the whole exercise epitomising the spirit-breaking tactics of the Nazis. It worked most efficiently, for the anxiety levels of the Jewish citizens of Sieradz had never been higher, balanced precariously like a trapeze artist on a single strand. He remembers only too vividly feeling sick in the pit of his stomach at the sight of totally unnecessary humiliating acts carried out by ordinary German soldiers, albeit by no means all of them, on the defenceless Jews. These occupying forces tormented middle-aged and older men by chopping off beards and tearing out their hair, even setting fire to some beards. These diabolical scenes confirmed the fact that the Hun had cart blanche to do to Jews whatever they wanted, with complete impunity.

The German soldiers were constantly humiliating the Jews and enjoying great amusement in doing so. Mayer remembered only too well the day they tormented young Famusz Kon, whose parents owned the ironmongery shop in Ulica Zamkowa (Castle Street). The soldiers made him run for his life with the threat of shooting him in the back more than once, each time firing over his head or to his side. The lad was petrified, metaphorically dying a death many times that day. Famusz survived that terrifying experience, and subsequently the camps, to eventually emigrate to Canada, a happy ending to his participation in this Jewish lottery of life.

On a lighter note, there was a Jewish family living on the ground floor of the flats in an annexe adjoining the main building and situated at the rear. These people were brilliant musicians and, soon after the occupation, their talents were recognised by a Wehrmacht soldier who, for a while, became a regular caller bringing food for the family and basking in the quality of their music. On one occasion on his arrival he noticed Yakov running barefoot out into the street. The next time the German came, this appreciator of good music and obviously a good-hearted man, gave Yakov a new pair of boots. Not all the occupying forces were hearts of stone Nazis.

Mayer's father and elder brother, Yakov, were taken to the army barracks and forced to water the horses. His father, tiring noticeably from carrying the great number of heavy buckets of water, stumbled on the stable yard and consequently was beaten brutally by a guard. On arriving home blood was pouring from his head and face. The image of what the future held for Jews was becoming ever clearer, a spine chilling picture of his father he can never forget.

Fifty men of the town were put away in prison on one occasion as hostages, all fifty being professional people including doctors, dentists and teachers. They were kept there for a number of days. Another group of people were selected from the streets to dig a mass grave at the Jewish cemetery, not knowing whether or not this grave was for themselves, for the Germans frequently made victims dig their own graves before eliminating them. As soon as the grave was completed the fifty professional people were lined up on the edge of the huge hole and they were shot. One of the professionals amazingly was still alive and tugged at the trouser leg of his friend, twenty year old David, whispering quietly, "how can you bury your friend alive?". David had to proceed to bury his friend for, if he had not, both friends would have been shot and buried. Nevertheless, the reaction this question had on David was slowly to send him insane and he was not to survive the Holocaust.

This occupation was not simply to be about life and death, but also constant acute mental trauma and torment for the survivors, day in day out, month in month out for a period of time, the length of which they knew not.

Further restrictions were brought in with respect to Jewish

people, no longer were they allowed to travel outside their confined area, nor were they able to pursue their professional career or trade. Food was very severely rationed and the only work one was allowed to do was slave labour without pay. Since few had money and food was so minimal, health and strength were soon on the decline with privation setting in very early.

As had already happened in Zdunska Wola and Zloczew, a ghetto was eventually formed in Sieradz in or around January 1940. Such an area was always centred on the most deprived area of the town. This ghetto catered for all the five thousand Jews of Sieradz, plus farming families from villages in surrounding areas. This most deprived area included Mayer's family home and the look of total fear in his parents' faces was a sight that will haunt him all his days. Whole families were fingerprinted and crowded into one room and, in days when families were large, this could mean ten and more people in an exceedingly confined space. They had no running water, no sewage system and fresh water had to be brought from a pump one hundred and fifty yards away, the Herszkowicz's position on the second floor made life harder, for dirty water and foul waste had to be taken out the same way. All the time people were being deported, with those from the middle classes being first, the reason for this being the Nazis not only wanted their lives, they also wanted their possessions. As soon as a family was taken away a seal was put on their door which decreed, in German and Polish, that if anyone broke that seal they would be executed. Subsequently the Germans would arrive with sophisticated magnetic machines to search for any valuables, took away anything they wanted, for instance furniture, and allowed non Jews to take any remaining goods that were surplus to the conqueror's requirements. The Third Reich overlooked nothing in their economic blitzkrieg that in any way would help its war effort. No stone was left unturned in the pursuit of bounty to feed Berlin.

In the ghetto, a German commandant was photographed with a man Mayer knew quite well, by the name of Hersz Majer Kliscienko, and always when on film the pitiful Jews were told to smile. Kliscienko was a glazier by trade, a very poor man who had ten children, one of whom was in Mayer's class, but nevertheless he was a very contented and cheery man who was always singing. He was never an envious man and this came through in his joyful vocal renderings. When the Germans first heard him sing they got hold of him and secured him to the roof of a tall local building in what was a very cold winter, they made him sing, and never allowed him to get down from his perch until he froze to death. Next morning German soldiers were shouting at the then limp figure suspended from the chimney stack to start singing again, laughing derisively as they did so. This mindless mockery of life only served to deepen the anxiety and the gloom that had descended on the Jews of Sieradz. The son of Kliscienko, who was the same age as Mayer, did not survive, being taken for forced labour, he and his family were transported on the Chelmno gassing route to meet their maker. Luck played a tremendously important role in the survival stakes, Mayer was well developed for his age whilst poverty had decreed that the Kliscienko boy was visibly not capable of withstanding hard labour.

With respect to the partisans, Mayer surprised me by stating that Jews were not even welcome to these 'fighters against tyranny' in these early weeks of occupation, despite having so much in common. Such was the anti-Semitic feeling at that time in Sieradz. He went on to further qualify this particular subject by explaining that further east in Russia, Jews did fight alongside partisans and also in certain other parts of Poland, although in the latter cases many were still discriminated against, referred to once again as 'dirty Jews'. He had been told that, in certain cases, Jews had been killed by partisans alongside whom they fought. During the latter stages of the conflict, when the final solution was comparatively common knowledge to the masses, Jews were more readily accepted by partisan groups.

The Jewish Committee was formed in order to convey the Nazi orders to their own local population, one member of this committee lived in the same block of flats as the Herszkowicz family. Most Jews were not too enamoured with the committee, thinking they were allowing themselves to be used by the occupying power to make conditions easier to enslave their own people. To others the absence of the Committee would have meant direct action from the Germans, which may have caused the situation to be even worse. These were primitive times indeed for there were no lights and a visit to the toilet down the yard entailed the use of a candle, the flame from which could well be extinguished by the wind. Mayer's father still worked from home in the ghetto and even on the market and, with the Germans relishing corduroy trousers and it not being in their nature to haggle on price, business was good. Corduroy material was only obtainable from Kalisz and this was where the enterprising and fearless Kajla helped her father greatly.

Even though it was not permitted, Kajla went on three occasions to Kalisz by train, wrapping the cloth around her body, and travelling home the same way, although, on one occasion, returning on the back of a German motorbike! The latter instance might sound somewhat surprising but Kajla was both pretty and blond and in all probability looked more German than the German soldier. Besides, the Germans were not known for raping the local girls, the Ukrainians being the worst for indulging in this vile practice. This practice of smuggling in cloth was extremely dangerous with an element of high-risk and she was forced to stop at her father's insistence. Profitable trade was desirable, but not at the risk of losing his one and only daughter.

In order to appreciate the degree that the Jewish race was the one preferentially selected by the Third Reich to be abused, humiliated and ultimately exterminated, one only had to be acquainted with the German work rules appertaining to the conquered masses. No Jews were ever called for use as forced labour. Non-Jews would fall into this work category and they would be paid and given tolerable food rations. Jews were only used as unpaid slave labour and given the most meagre of rations, meagre enough in most cases to ensure the Jew died, for the Aryan masters wanted but two things from this afflicted race, useful work and ultimate death. Non-Jews doing the same job were housed in a different camp, a better camp, they were paid for their time and received a far superior quality and quantity of food.

Shortly after the ghetto was formed an excellent tailor by the name of Bloom moved into one of the first floor flats and Mayer's father asked the newcomer if he could take his son, Mayer, on as an apprentice. This new relationship started well with Bloom enjoying good business from the Germans, particularly in relation to the sewing of new insignia, often caused by promotions in the ranks. Mayer learnt to sew these onto the very stiff uniform collars, physically very demanding with respect to strength in the hands. The work had to be done perfectly, for the Germans were exceedingly particular when it came to their uniforms looking smart, sometimes the soldiers giving a tip and sometimes not. This useful business did not last long however for soon all Germans were forbidden to give work to Jews. This decree was a hammer blow to any hopes Jews might have had of a 'reasonable' war, as had happened in the 1914-18 encounter. They were Germans, these were German Nazis and the differences were not lost on the Jewish sector even at this early stage. Bloom was better off than the average Jew because he was a top tailor in both ladies and gents clothes. Mayer was to be unfortunate enough to witness one of Bloom's sons, a tall lad, later brutally beaten to death in the Lusenheim camp.

After the occupation started Mayer tended to stay in the house more, whereas his elder brother, Yakov, would hang about the streets. One day he paid the penalty for this decision when the Germans rounded him, and other Jews, up and marched them out of the ghetto. This action brought great distress to their parents and they were relieved indeed to see him return later that night but they recoiled at the stench that accompanied him. Yakov had spent many hours cleaning out cesspits!

As life in the ghetto continued the non-appearance of farmers fetching their products meant food was getting more and more scarce. Jews were allowed a limited number of bread coupons only, there was no butter and only a small amount of molasses available. The food shortage was further exasperated by the fact that Jews were not allowed to follow their trade and work, hence their earnings were nil and therefore they were always short of cash. Anyone who had spare cash or could sell some possession fared slightly better, but most struggled horrendously on the miserly, German controlled rations, many living from hand to mouth. Black market activities did occur, he remembered his father managing to sell some pairs of trousers made before the full restrictions were applied. Unlike the ghettos of Lodz and Warsaw, this one was not hermetically sealed and therefore such sales would necessitate leaving the ghetto and re-entering it later. Such activities, however, attracted public beatings or hangings or both. Stark hunger in one's children persuaded some to take the ultimate risk. Although starvation inevitably arrived in the ghetto, the quantity and choice of food was to be infinitely better than that about to be experienced by Mayer throughout his five years and two months of hard labour and extermination camp survival. Comparative luxuries like potatoes, bread and molasses gave the ghetto a decided advantage, the latter being available from a sugar refinery in Sieradz which was a stroke of luck for the beleaguered Jews of the town. Being a small community, and living near numerous farms, meant that they were better off than large cities like Lodz and Warsaw, where life was so miserable that when these ghettos were evacuated, Mayer believed the people would move without too much resistance, for what misery could be worse than that they'd just experienced. This constituted clever mind games on the part of the Germans, ensuring smooth transportation of millions to their point of liquidation.

The police kept law and order in the town and, in addition,

possessed the official list of names and ages for slave labour purposes. Very few women were put to forced labour. Yakov was told to report to the town police station and was deported to Rawicz, situated on the old pre war German/Polish border, from where he sent heavily censored letters. The occupying forces took photographs of every Jew deported and every one killed. Wanda Turowiczowa, a Polish non-Jew, was the pharmacist at the chemist shop in Market Square, a mere fifty to seventy yards from Mayer's street. Her assistant was Henryka Szturme, also a Polish non-Jew, who ran the photographic side of the shop and it was he who ensured that the outside world might have an insight into how life was under the Nazis. The risks he took were indeed great but that extra print copy he stored, in most cases of excellent quality, will help modern generations understand more and pull the ground from under those who still maintain the Holocaust never in effect happened. Some of these German photographs accompany Mayer's account, thereby lending further authenticity to those most emotional of times.

Mayer remembered four names on the Jewish Committee, Knopf, Henochowicz and Katz were members of the Jewish police formed by the Germans, and Rosenbaum was a successful businessman. The latter was asked by the SS to name one hundred Jews for slave labour, to which he said that he was unable to do that because he did not know that many. The SS officer gave him a plain piece of paper and told him to put his own name on top of the list. He thus was sent to hard labour and was the only member of the Jewish Committee to survive the war, Yakov confirmed, after the conflict was over, that he had lived to see freedom. Unfortunately this brave man died in a road accident, after the war, somewhere in Germany. Yakov and Rosenbaum shared the same camp more than once during their years of persecution and he believed the year of his friend's death to be 1947. The members of the Jewish Committee must have considered that they had a job until the end of hostilities but, in effect, although none of them were sent to a labour camp, it was part of the perverse Nazi humour that their survival was never intended, and they were all simply murdered at the whim of the SS.

Eventually all new arrivals into the ghetto stopped and by this time very few able bodied Jews remained. Roll call was still twice a day, taking place in a square towards the river, since the market square was outside the ghetto perimeter. The Jews would be vociferously goaded into leaving their pitiful dwellings, liberally laced with brutality, their spirits by now totally crushed, the river acting as a barrier to any with escape attempts in mind. On these occasions, and to further rub salt into already stinging wounds, the non-Jewish population would loot the Jewish homes. These so called Christians could not even wait for the Jews to be killed, an attitude he considered insensitive at the very least and distinctively presumptuous. Nevertheless he had to admit that non-Jews had access to more information than his own oppressed race, who were told absolutely nothing. Christians, many of whom drove the doomed to their place of extermination, were aware that Jews were to be totally exterminated, and probably thought no opportunity for material gain should be wasted.

Before the ghetto was formed, farmers would come around the area with produce to sell but, after its formation, any non-Jew entering, for the ghetto was not sealed, would be hanged. As a matter of interest, in Zdunska Wola when a non-Jew entered the ghetto for a suit, both he and the Jew were hanged, photographs were taken before and during hanging. The Germans never missed an opportunity to crush the Jews' spirit by publicising executions and maximising degradation.

The first people to be deported from Mayer's block of flats was the landlord, Sonheim, and his family. Sonheim, who did a lot of business with the farmers of the region, was a tall and much respected man in Sieradz, having a large, and also extended, family. Indeed, when the family left, there remained an elderly lady on the first floor, believed to be his aunt.

From the end of October 1939 Heinrich Himmler decreed that during the ensuing three months all Jews had to be cleared out of the rural areas of western Poland, in the Poznan region no less than fifty communities were affected. One of the smaller villages, by the name of Chelmno, contained only thirty three Jews, all of which were immediately deported to the poor village region between Lublin and Nisko, the so-called 'Lubinland reservation'. A little over a year later their tiny inconspicuous village became the site of the first death camp. The first gassing at Chelmno took place on the 8th December 1941. It was judged a success, and its use and infamy grew out of all proportion. In the middle of September 1942 the SS decided to make the Lodz ghetto a strictly 'working' ghetto by launching the 'Gehsperre' action, that was one strictly controlled by curfew regulations. Consequently Chelmno was entrusted with the extermination of all children below ten years of age and men and women over sixty. Sixteen thousand Jews in these age groups had their ashes scattered on the bed of the River Ner in a period of less than two weeks. Around the 12th January 1945 the Russian forces started to make their big push toward the heart of Germany and, as they did so, Chelmno was coming to the end of its useful life. By then it only contained forty seven Jewish slave labourers who, knowing that they were about to be shot by the SS as the Soviets drew closer, revolted, using a building to hold out in. The SS set fire to the building and machine gunned those who fled from it. Their brave unarmed resistance, by a stroke of good fortune, enabled a positive result to be obtained, one of the forty seven survived. Yet another, by giving factual evidence about the efficiently evil Chelmo operation, to bear witness to the world that the Holocaust was not just a figment of Jewish imaginations.

With regard to the Jewish deportations from the town, women were very rarely sent to even a slave labour camp but were killed on arrival at their destination, usually Chelmno. In fact, Mayer's mother and three younger brothers, Hershel, Chaim Alter and Tovia, the youngest of whom was only seven years old, were all deported around the end of August 1942. They were first incarcerated in the cloister in the town. In all four thousand of them were held for four and a half days without food or water and without toilet facilities. From there they were taken to Kolo, only 5 kms from Chelmno, and into a specially adapted church, from which all pews had been removed and one side had been opened up with direct access to the gassing vans, from which all pews had been removed and one side had been opened up with direct access to the gassing vans. In this sacred place they were forced to get undressed and hand over all their personal belongings such as wedding rings and forced into a gassing van, where in all probability they would all be dead in about fifteen minutes. These gassing vans appeared to be ambulances, adorned as they were with a red cross, yet another German ruse, but in fact they were specially constructed vehicles with a contrastingly different purpose. The naked Jews were forced into these vans until full when the doors were securely fastened. A coupling was connected allowing the carbon monoxide exhaust gases back into the inside of the vehicle, this method of elimination having the distinct added advantage of simultaneously moving the corpses to the site of disposal. One might think this method of extermination of Jews would be slow and far from efficient in use. One would be wrong in this belief for, from the Germans' own records, over a period of six months just three of these so called 'gassing vans' killed no less than ninety seven thousand Jews. Without doubt this was industrialised mass murder.

His voice choked with emotion, Mayer proceeded to explain that the gassing in these red cross marked vans typified the dedicated organisation and ruthless efficiency of the Nazi order, held in high esteem by one of its hierarchy connected with the final solution of the Jewish problem, none other than Adolf Eichmann himself. This evil administrator paid a visit to Chelmno and witnessed the unloading of one van where some of the victims were still alive and 'twitching'. This sight offended the mass murderer and brought the comment from him, 'this makes me feel sick!' At this time the Germans were experiencing some problems with the tilting of the vans, especially when the vehicles were not completely full. It was suggested by the Chelmno engineers that a smaller floor area to the van would assist in greater packing density and consequently an absence of movement. Reports on this issue were sent to the German manufacturer of the vans, Sauer, with a copy to Berlin, the latter still being kept in German archives.

Eichmann was a ruthless implementer of the final solution and there can be no better example of his dedication to the cause than shortly after the annexation of Austria when the efficient organiser of death was in civilian clothes sitting at an open air cafe in Vienna. Nazi bully boys approached and started beating him up and calling him a dirty Jew. The reason was his long nose and other typically Jewish facial features. Eichmann reacted angrily for his nose had placed him in similar situations as early as his days at Linz High School in Austria. He pointed out that he was not a Jew and, in fact, was a superior Nazi to them because he was an SS man, but unfortunately he had no proof of this on his person. The young thugs laughed derisively and a brawl ensued which came to the attention of the Austrian Nazi Party who interviewed Eichmann intensely and thoroughly investigated the antecedents of his grandparents, an investigation that continued as late as 1934. Sometime later he made it his business to seek out the youths and showed them his Nazi membership card, going on to tell them that he wasn't annoyed and, in fact, was very proud of them for their action! Eichmann's hatred of the Jews bordered on mania and his total dedication to their complete extermination, as important to him as winning the war, can be gauged from a quotation of his made before his own death in Israel in the early sixties. *'I shall leap into my grave laughing, because the feeling that I have the deaths of five million people on my conscience will be for me a source of extraordinary satisfaction'.*

The ghetto population was continuing to be reduced in size by the steady shipping of Jews deemed fit for slave labour and indeed Mayer's elder brother, Yakov, was told in December 1939 to report to the police station as he was required for work. He left somewhat hurriedly leaving behind a good quality pair of boots, the family waving him off and not knowing for certain whether or not he would be back that night. The Herszkowicz family accepted his departure as part and parcel of the oppression and persecution of the day but, nevertheless, hoped he would be working locally as he had done previously and therefore be able to keep in touch. They each clung to their misguided belief that, since he was going to work for the Germans, he should be in receipt of more food than the miserly rations available in the ghetto. One great advantage the ghetto afforded, however, was the supportive strength of one's family and, providing an individual was willing to keep off the streets, avoidance of forced labour could, to some extent, be achieved. His father told Mayer that he would be next and so it transpired that in March 1940, in the middle of the night, there was a knock on the door answered by his mother. An armed German soldier and a policeman read out Mayer's name and he was told to get dressed immediately and accompany them. It was sometime after midnight and, with their one room accommodating all the family, everyone was awake and experienced the frightening drama of the moment. His mother helped him get ready, packing a few things she thought might prove useful, including the good pair of boots left by Yakov and a blanket. Mayer never said goodbye to his father for fear of attracting attention to the head of the household, in case he might be seized as well. This omission, although born of good intentions, has left him with a deep feeling of guilt which he still feels to this day. The German soldier impatiently gesticulated with his rifle, not even allowing thirteen year old Mayer the time to express the most basic of human feelings for his beloved family. He never said goodbye to his younger brothers or his elder sister Kajla. The Nazi oppressors never saw fit to display any sign of civilised behaviour. Mayer at this time felt totally bewildered, not knowing where he was going, to a labour camp or even to his own imminent execution. Even if they gave factual information as to one's destination, you would be foolish to give the statement any credence, for the Germans would sometimes give false good news in order to encourage co-operation from prisoners, giving a smooth transfer and less hassle for themselves. He was frightened and completely in the dark. His mother hugged him with tears in her eyes, wondering if they were ever going to see each other again. Of course, they never did.

At the moment of parting Mayer believed that working for the Germans should at least yield slightly more food than the pitifully minimal quantities then available in the ghetto. Looking back, and in hindsight, he believes his family, at that time, shared the same opinion. Nevertheless, if given the choice, he desperately wanted to stay, for the strength gained from the love of his family was irreplaceable. Little did he know that his thoughts on food supply whilst working could be so far from the truth, for not only did the Germans want them to work, they wanted them to die also, there being no shortage of more Jews available for unpaid slave labour.

Chapter Four

He left his family and, together with other men, was force marched into the huge prison in Sieradz, well known nationally and which served an extremely large area. It had fairly recently been even further enlarged by the addition of an annex, and it was in this brand new section that Mayer found himself in the company of his best school friend, David Josefowicz, and 25 year old Pietruska, a family man with two children, who was a good friend of Mayer's elder brother, Yakov, and shoe repairer to the Herszkowicz family. Mayer was amazed at the number of very young boys like himself who were in the party, clearly indicating the fact that their hosts were experiencing a shortage of adults for forced labour. They were kept overnight in a packed prison cell, attempting to sleep on the concrete floor, with just a bucket as a toilet facility. Mayer remembering his incredible amazement at this barbaric facility in such an extremely smart new gaol complex. Compared to what the future held, he was not to know that this new annex was tantamount to four-star accommodation.

Mayer was used to enjoying a good night's sleep and even this first disturbed and distraught night had had a marked effect on his general well being. Early in the morning they were marched to the local barracks where they underwent a make believe medical examination from a German doctor in order to check their fitness for hard labour and to try to fool people into thinking that the Germans really cared about them, the whole process being pure theatre from start to finish. In an attempt to keep the Jews as calm and as peaceful as possible, the Germans would announce that this was their last transportation, although, in hindsight, this could have been a perversely sarcastic sense of humour for many, unable to take any more, turned to suicide for merciful relief. Next morning they were taken to the railway station where they were crammed into cattle trucks and set off in a north/north west direction for approximately 90 kms to the first slave labour camp. Not one of the highly apprehensive prisoners knew to where they were going or what they would be expected to do and this total unawareness heightened everyone's fears. There was not a picture window through which one might assess to where they were headed and, in fact, the only vision afforded to one inmate at a time was a crack in the timbers of their conveyance. There was neither food nor water provided and full toilet facilities consisted merely of a bucket. Since this was everyone's first slave labour conveyance, the conditions were viewed as distinctly harsh and few could have perceived just how unimaginably horrendous future transits were to become. As soon as the train stopped, after at least four hours travel and the sliding doors were flung open, the fifty men could see the name of their destination, the camp Otoczno, later to be spelt in the German fashion, Otoschno. On the platform stood the welcoming committee comprising SS guards with horse whips. All hell broke loose immediately, deliberately designed to demoralise the Jews, their hosts screaming "heraus! heraus! schneller! schneller!, beating the slaves brutally and forcing them to deposit every belonging they had with them on the platform. Thus Mayer lost the blanket and clothing given to him by his mother. He was later to

45

reflect that probably the Germans had allowed them to keep their possessions thus far in order to convince prisoners that their conqueror's intentions might be construed as reasonable. This was the first time in his life that Mayer had been on the business end of a horse whip and he found it a most humiliating and degrading experience inflicting considerable pain. The Germans' high-pitched screaming, which was to become a constant feature throughout all his camp travels, was done in order to demoralise prisoners and eventually to persuade them to succumb to every German order given. The Nazis were to prove extremely skilled in breaking the human spirit. This introduction to German hospitality immediately made him consider that, if they treated prisoners of use to them in this way, what hideous treatment awaited those of no material use to the cause of the Third Reich? They marched into the camp which consisted of about ten barracks, there was no furniture there, no heating and the guard told them they must not talk to each other. They thought he was joking, but the guard would listen in behind the closed door and, as soon as he heard any whispering, he would fling the door open and would ask them who was talking. Nobody came forward and consequently all were forced out to be given collective punishment, ten strokes of a very thick belt each on the backside. The recipients could not sit or lie on their backs for quite a few days, such was the pain inflicted. Each prisoner that first night received his food ration consisting merely of four ounces of hard, stale dry bread.

I had already agreed with Mayer that I would ask him questions as and when they came to mind rather than risk forgetfulness and the loss of this informational tool.

"Considering the fact that you have already stated you did not have the physical appearance of a Jew, did you ever consider trying to conceal your Jewish identity?"

"No, I was proud to be a Jew. I was brought up in a good orthodox Jewish family, amidst sincerity, honesty, charity and love. The Germans defined a Jew as having two Jewish grandparents out of the four providing that Jew belonged to the Jewish religion or was married to another Jew. Even if a Jew's parents were converted to Christianity, he or she would still fall foul of the Nazi grandparent rule. Half-Jews and one-quarter Jews, those descended from one Jewish grandparent, who did not practice Judaism were lumped together in a new non-Aryan racial category created by the decree Mischlinge, meaning mixed race."

The barracks at Otoczno were laid out in a square configuration, the enclosed area being used for roll call and, while the camp was not hermetically sealed and escape was therefore possible, it was never a realistic option for the starving Jews who had neither money, papers nor energy, the latter being worked and beaten out of them. It was a brand new camp with the men sleeping on the floor with a little straw and they even had to build their own barbed wire fence, together with hauling extremely heavy sleepers to put down on the large expanse of a sea of mud.

They each received the basic food ration which consisted of a quarter pound of bread, or 125 grams, in the evening once a day plus also a little watery soup. Knowing that he would not receive any more food for twenty four hours, Mayer broke part of his bread off and put it in one of his boots, the pair of them constituting his pillow. When he woke up in the morning there was no bread left. A neighbour

47

of his was a little bit hungrier than Mayer. He never made that mistake again, food was to be eaten there and then when you had it, circumstances decreed that the thirteen year old boy was a man before he was fourteen.

"With food being at such a premium for survival, did anybody in the camps treat you any better due to you being younger? For instance with, possibly, a little extra food?"

"No, they could not spare anything. I couldn't blame them, for everyone just wanted to survive."

They all had to rise at 3.30 in the morning, immediately on the sound of the whistle; they did not have to dress because they always slept in their camp clothing. They were forced to quickly go to the latrine by the use of whips, whilst another guard in the latrine was whipping them to get out immediately, without time for washing. Roll call then took place together with the offering of some artificial tea prior to moving off to work. Their first day in the camp saw them making a barbed wire fence, they carried very heavy railway sleepers which were sodden with water and Mayer was lifting these with a man much older than himself, in his twenties and much taller than he, leaving all the weight on Mayer's shoulder. He knew he could not carry it much further and soon he dropped it. Not far behind was a big nineteen year old German foreman, name of Rudi, who came from the Sudatenland, Czechoslovakia, a nasty brute who accused Mayer's colleague of dropping the sleeper and consequently the latter received a very severe beating. The two slaves struggled to shoulder the sleeper again and this time Rudi walked alongside Mayer, who, minutes later, dropped the weight again. The foreman started to thrash

Mayer unmercifully about the face and neck with a thin whip, a most painful experience, but, since he was fresh from home and a good runner, Mayer ran away from his aggressor, comfortably outpacing him and escaping his clutches. Rudi left him alone, the reason being there was plenty of surplus labour that day.

The following day there followed a similar timetable, marched out at five am and present at the workplace at six am. They collected their pick axe, shovel and spade and learned they were about to start to build a massive new railway system from scratch, originating in Germany and running deep into Poland. Of course none of them had had previous experience but in charge of it were highly skilled German civilian engineers who would supervise it from beginning to end. Come half past nine the German civilians had their second breakfast, but the Jews received nothing. Come twelve o'clock they had their lunch yet the Jews could not even get a drop of water. At six pm when it was time to march back to camp some of his colleagues could not walk unaided, some were so exhausted from their labours whilst others were badly injured and some were already dead. The beatings they received from the foremen or some of the German civilian engineers were always harsh and usually bordered on the extreme. Carrying heavy equipment back to the camp was a supreme test of strength for the weakened Jews and roll call would see some standing and others collapsed close to death. Providing the numbers tallied to those who had left the camp that morning, that was all the German officers were concerned about. When numbers dropped as they did regularly, they were replaced by newcomers who were initially bombarded by questions from the inmates with respect to news of any of the latter's relatives, but, with replies always in the negative, afterwards there was little else to talk about.

Although Mayer's natural game plan for survival was always to be predominately one of caution and an absence of unnecessary risk taking, in these his relatively early days of forced labour, he was already beginning to feel the savage pangs of hunger brought about by the miniscule rations of substances more akin to pig swill than human food. In one incident, whilst walking past the SS kitchens, he noticed some bones laying in the mud, probably thrown out for the German dogs. Tentatively glancing around to check the absence of Nazi shadows, he reached a snap decision to smash the bones and extract the marrow, beneficial whether in the raw or cooked state. His decision was supported by his expertise with an axe, perfected over a few years of chopping wood back at home. Unfortunately there was no axe to hand, so instead he grabbed at the first brick he saw, splintering the bones against a stout sleeper. In his frenzied haste not to be seen, he caught one of his fingers a vicious blow and, even to this day, he has no feeling in that fingertip. He did extract a small amount of marrow but did not continue any longer for fear of being caught, realising the immense risk he had taken. He never remembered seeing any bones in any other camp but, had there been any, they would always have been near the SS kitchens. Beads of sweat crowded his brow as he imagined what may have befallen him should he have been discovered in the act. Although still a comparatively 'green' rookie in terms of surviving captivity, young Jews learnt quickly in those dark days of repression and he was acutely aware that the very least punishment he would receive would be the severest of floggings in front of many fellow prisoners and then, no doubt, equally publicly, hanged as an example of the extreme reprisals meted out to the race the Germans simply did not want to survive.

One day Mayer was taken with some others to work on a farm where one would imagine food would be reasonably plentiful. It was but not for Jews. The foreman would watch them like a hawk but there came a time when that foreman had to go for his sandwiches, when the Jews took advantage by jumping into the pig pen and taking some of the pig swill. Although there was plenty of grit in it and other muck, Mayer had never enjoyed food as much as on that occasion, such was the degree of hunger he was experiencing at that time. Had they been caught, they would have been executed by hanging. This did in fact happen when they were working near a village and some of their number were tempted to knock on a door and ask for food. Some of them were caught on the way back, or were informed against, when they would receive a very severe flogging prior to being flung into the camp dungeons where they would be deprived of food and water. On this occasion the Germans assembled no less than 52 of these people who had committed this so called crime. Eventually on the day that the mass execution was announced all the slave labourers were forced to watch their friends, schoolmates, neighbours and relatives being hung. Two of them were reprieved because, according to German law, nobody under fourteen years of age could be hung. They could be starved to death, beaten to death or even thrown into a gassing van but not hung. One of the two reprieved was David Josefowitz, that very good school friend of Mayer's who died in 1997. They had to watch with their eyes fixed on this horrible spectacle for anyone allowing their eyes to wander from the scene was beaten unmercifully and the SS told them, "let this be a warning to you". Mayer witnessed many such executions during his five years and two months, only the number of victims being eliminated varied.

His friend was named David Josefowicz and he actually did escape and reached his home town of Sieradz on foot where he was immediately recognised by a policeman. 'I know who you are, you're a dirty Jew', the officer of the law venomously spat out and proceeded to give young David a severe beating prior to organising his return to Otoczno. The net result of this exercise only served to support Mayer's opinion that the odds against a successful, sustainable escape were so preposterous, the gamble was not worth a second thought.

One day whilst working alone with a non Jewish Pole, Mayer was asked why he didn't try to escape since his colleague reckoned he in no way looked Jewish. Mayer retorted thoughtfully, "I have no papers, my clothes are so ragged I would soon be recognised and captured, for there are plenty of informers about, plenty of people willing to betray a Jew for even small reward. Where would I shelter and who would give me refuge, besides some of my colleagues have tried but not succeeded." The odds against escape seemed insurmountable.

Another method to reduce the number of Jews was to perform a selection process to determine who was going to die that day, those being considered were already emaciated due to starvation and hard work. The SS would come along and pick out the worst looking cases which were described as beschrenkt, a German word he only ever heard at the railway camps, meaning limited, and the gassing van was waiting just a few yards away for its next consignment. Since the victims knew what was going to happen to them, they were all very reluctant to get into that death vehicle. Consequently sticks, clubs and whips were brought out and used brutally on these pathetic slaves, so much so that blood was pouring from their heads, yet those wretches had to get into the van. None were ever seen again.

Considering the intensely physical nature of the work, Mayer realised that to stand any chance of survival, food was absolutely vital, especially since the thin watery soup merely consisted of Kulrabi, a field crop grown exclusively for cows. Again this was another humiliation for Jews to suffer, much to the amusement of the guards, an entire race being treated worse than animals. Since many objects were being stolen, Mayer decided to sell his new boots for a loaf of bread. The boots did in fact belong to Yakov who had inadvertently left them in his sudden departure to the labour camp.

This first camp seemed like hell on earth with reveille as early as 3.30 am and the only break any of them received was when they had bones broken during brutal beatings from foremen, guards and even some of the civilian engineers. Marching back to camp the fit men had to carry these pathetic victims with broken arms or legs on their shoulders. The Germans had carte blanche to do to Jews whatever they wanted for there was no redress for over the top brutality. In the daily queue for ultra thin soup, the German guards would play games by chasing Jews who had got their soup, they'd run and spill their precious lifeline by overbalancing on the sleepers. There was no refill facility available at this workplace.

Adjacent to the Jewish camp, and totally separate from

it, was a non-Jewish camp where inmates wallowed in such luxuries as potatoes, margarine and even some meat. It was tempting for the Jews to visit their rubbish bins and pick up potato peelings, an incredible luxury but carrying huge risk.

The non-Jews did not go through the ultimate torment, the selection process, unlike Mayer and company. Those fit only for gassing were selected by SS officers in blue and grey uniforms and those unfortunates were then passed on to the gassing van guards. Most Jews were worn out from work but those who showed reluctance to enter the van were beaten unmercifully with blood pouring from them. To many it was a relief and possibly a better way out, for there were many who just couldn't take anymore. Those gassing van victims were all buried or burnt in Chelmno, forty kms from Otoczno, and renamed by the Germans as Kulmhof.

During the first three to four weeks at Otoczno their hosts allowed the prisoners to send a card home to their families, this being the only time this concession was ever made during Mayer's marathon of misery through nine camps. He received a reply from his sister, Kajla, but was so choked with emotion that he asked Pietruska, a good friend who played in goal for the same football team as Yakov, to read it to him. Pietruska, probably in his mid twenties in 1940 and married with at least two children, lived in the same street as Mayer a few blocks distant, and was a jovial chap who made shoes for the Herszkowicz family and knew them all very well. He read what was probably a heavily censored letter in which Kajla wrote, 'I go to make the bed and there is no bed to make'. This brief disguised sentence revealed the encapsulated fears that she and the rest of the family had and how desperately worried they were and how they missed both Mayer and Yakov. Mayer could not read these letters nor write replies to them, because he was too choked with emotion. That good friend, Pietruska, penned a reply, for all that Mayer could do was to stumble over a few heartfelt phrases. He was a true rock for the thirteen year old, assuring him that everything would one day be alright again, a sentiment deep down he knew was no more than wishful thinking, but nevertheless saying and doing everything he could to bolster the boy's spirit.

The SS and the ethnic German guards wore an all black uniform and seemed to compete against each other to see who could sink to the lowest level of depravity when dealing with the two hundred or so Jewish slave labourers at Otoczno.

Two or three Jewish foremen were appointed and Mayer, who always had to pretend to be older than he was, tended to be wary of them lest they betray his true age. The Germans were cunning indeed when they would ask the young ones if they wanted to go home. It was a trick and if the question caught a youngster unawares and he answered in the affirmative, he would either be eliminated on the spot or taken home from where the lad and his parents would be put to the gassing vans.

Mayer worked more than once with a Polish Jew named Szczupak, a few years older than himself and hailing from a small community just outside Sieradz, whose nature it was to always take chances, rather than play safe, and risk all in the name of gain. On this particular occasion the two worked on a job alone and a friendly engineer from Frankfurt approached Mayer, asking him where his friend was and suggesting that he might again be in the toilet.

Mayer nodded in agreement and the German shook his head and warned Szczupak later that if he caught him missing again without the foreman's permission, he would report him to the SS. The work was so hard and the conditions so deplorable that just half a minute in the toilet was an enormous relief, a rest to catch your breath. When totally starved, man is a zombie and his brain doesn't function properly. Survivors would leave sufficient mental energy to last through that day, that hour or even that minute as they responded to the whistle and the whip. It was incredible how so much work could be done by skeletal men on virtually no food working seven days a week. Not much later Szczupak, unable to change his habits, took one chance too many and was caught and hanged.

On one particularly obnoxious job the Germans enjoyed using Jews and that was the emptying of the cesspits into tankers and then harnessing teams of them to the tanker like horses, the guard on top making liberal use of the whip to force them to drag the heavy tanker away.

Arriving back at the barracks at night, they were allowed to talk to each other until curfew which was at 8.30pm. A prized possession for the Jews was a soup bowl, which was never washed but always licked clean. Its owner would keep it with him at all times, even on his person at work, for fear it would be stolen whilst labouring on the railroad. One or two lucky ones may even possess in addition a spoon. The Germans had a golden rule, no bowl, no soup. In the morning after latrines their bowls would hold a small volume of lukewarm chicory, no food would be given and, after roll call, the prisoners faced twelve hours of incredibly hard labour. In the evening, roll call preceded a hard piece of black bread and watery soup. Suddenly ghetto food in

Mayer's mind was elevated to the realms of comparative plentiful goodness.

A very good friend, Arek Hersh, who went to the same school as Mayer, fell for the German ruse and inadvertently volunteered to be sent home from Otoczno to his family, and consequently, he was bound for Chelmno and the gassing vans. It was an exceedingly hot day as they changed trains at Sieradz and, being very thirsty, Arek grabbed a pan and jumped outside the train to get some water. Here an SS guard accosted him and asked him which trade he followed. The answer, 'tailor', persuaded the guard to push him unceremoniously into the queue for the ghetto of Lodz with Mayer's father and sister Kajla. This incredible stroke of luck saved his life and enabled him to survive the war.

Chapter Five

As soon as the work from Otoczno had finished, surviving slaves were sent to the next camp at Lusenheim in order to build the continuation of the railway system. Again this camp was laid out in a square design but did boast one slight improvement, which meant sleeping in two tier bunk beds rather than on the barrack floor. They were initially employed in building marshalling yards and, when they were ready, Mayer was then given the job of selecting different wagons to feed into different lines by skilful use of the points, and stopping wagons with blocks of wood if they didn't have a brake. The size of wooden block was critical, for, if too large, derailment was possible. A chief engineer told them that if they made a mistake they would be executed. It was quite a skilful job and one had to be extremely quick in jumping on top of the wagon and slowing it down.

Since there was no running water in this camp they also had to bring in water from the next town by tanker, Mayer and others being harnessed to the tanker like horses. The guard would sit on the top with a whip and every so often he would indulge in his favourite sport of beating Jews. Anybody with decent shoes or boots ran a fair risk of having them stolen and consequently, by that time, Mayer had already sold his shoes for food and thus went to work barefooted. Shortly afterwards he managed to get a rusty nail in his heel but luckily removed it later, nevertheless that hole in his heel took a long time to heal, years in fact.

By a stroke of great fortune Mayer did not get tetanus or any other infection.

Many were getting near the end of their stamina and suicides were not uncommon. A man so lost in despair and who could see no light at the end of a seemingly endless tunnel would pull his shirt over his head, placing his neck on the line in front of the oncoming train. If the guard saw him in time he would stop him, screaming at him, 'you filthy Jew, you do not deserve to die so easily', and would then proceed to beat him brutally. Sometimes the guard would deliberately misjudge the intensity of such beating and he would quite intentionally extinguish the wretch's life there and then.

Lusenheim was the stage for one of the most barbaric happenings that Mayer personally witnessed. All the prisoners were forced to watch the beating of a tall young lad, a quiet good looking young man, about nineteen years of age, who was a son of that excellent tailor from Sieradz, Mr Bloom, to whom Mr Herszkowicz had hoped to apprentice Mayer, an arrangement curtailed by the German occupation. The boy had done nothing, they could have taken anybody to stand this sadistic treatment as a means to further break the spirit of the Jewish labourers. Not only was the attendance of all prisoners mandatory, but also their full attention to every horrific moment was insisted upon by the Nazis. The entire staged event was totally unnecessary for Jewish heads had well dropped by this stage. Two Germans with horse whips applied the punishment vigorously, ensuring as each lash cut the skin, the next was only a second or two away. To start with, the boy's screams accompanied each and every lash but soon he could scream no more as multitudes of blows, without respite, rained down on his whole back. It was a most inhumane sight as his lungs collapsed and he died. Such was the intensity of the beating, the whole staged production lasted only about ten minutes, his limp body left there as a warning to the rest of the inmates. The Germans excelled as breakers of the human spirit.

"One would assume Mayer that if you were a big, strong and fit Jew, would you not have a better chance of survival?"

"No, certainly not, in fact quite the contrary, because people who are big and strong needed more food and guards would beat them more heavily and expect them to do more work. Eventually this greater expectation and harsher treatment meant they would succumb earlier."

The party of Jews working with Mayer decided to bribe the ethnic German foreman not to beat them so hard. They could only do this by offering him cigarettes, which they obtained from non Jewish Poles, or German civilians, for food. The exchange did work for them but they could not do this often for they needed their miserly bread ration to try to survive. One day this same foreman picked on Mayer for no apparent reason, beatings were often for no obvious reason, and savagely set about him with a heavy wooden club and broke several ribs, these same ribs still being distorted to this day, for cracked ribs heal, but not when they're broken. Every time Mayer breathed he was in excruciating pain, which lasted a number of days before beginning to subside.

There were up to 300 Jews at Lusenheim and there was much excavation work going on, using big diggers, which unfortunately had no tracks and consequently had to be rolled on and off sleepers, which was a particularly exhausting task. Mayer and two others had to fill lorries with soil and the other two told the foreman that the boy Mayer could not do this heavy work. Good fortune smiled on Mayer that day for the ethnic German foreman replied that they would have to make up for the boy. This was particularly bad news for the other two because, should the daily allocation of work not be achieved, there would be severe beatings for all three responsible for the shortfall.

A neighbour of the Herszkowicz family worked in close proximity to Mayer in Lusenheim, a big strong man, qualities which unfortunately did not stand him in good stead in slave labour camps. His first name was Moniek and he was a schoolmate of Mayer's, although two years older. He came from a wonderful home, 9 Dressmaker Street, a comfortable middle class home where he had received the services of a nanny and was in receipt of a good education. Because he came from a more affluent upbringing, he suffered worse than most of the other prisoners. The bigger and stronger the Jew the more harsh the beating, as though it was a challenge to the foreman to break his spirit and bring him down to the pitiful levels of the wretches around him. Although a really good worker, for some unknown reason the foreman picked on him persistently and he perished at Lusenheim.

I had considered my next question most carefully but was somewhat taken aback at the answer.

"If you had been from a higher social class, would you have been treated any differently?"

"Yes, most certainly, for middle and upper classes would be murdered first of all, not for their bodies so much as their possessions, be they jewellery, cash or real estate."

One day, whilst Mayer was changing the points over in the marshalling yards, a member of the Hitler Youth appeared on top of a nearby embankment and shouted a greeting in German. It was immediately obvious to Mayer that the youth did not realise he was addressing a Jew, the reasons for this being firstly that he did not look like a Jew and secondly he was not wearing any telltale uniform, merely shirt, jacket and trousers. Mayer's German was good and the two chatted amicably before the youth mentioned that he had an uncle in Sieradz who walked with a limp and worked at the town hall. From this description Mayer instantly knew the man, whose job was a tax collector. The two boys were drawn closer together by this common denominator, especially with Mayer stating that he knew the person as a wonderful man. This was a white lie but absolutely permissible in the dire circumstances in which he found himself. Mentioning that he was very hungry brought an unexpected gift from the Hitler youth, nothing less than a raw potato, which was manna from heaven to Mayer. Scooping some hot cinders from the steam engine and using a little sand from the railway line, the youngster from Sieradz managed to bake a tasty potato. Next day the two lads met again and were getting on really well, this time his new friend was more generous with three potatoes. Mayer hadn't noticed the Chief Engineer approaching and unfortunately he had seen everything. The engineer turned sternly toward the Hitler youth, 'if I see you feeding a Jew again I'll report it to the SS. Did you not know it was totally forbidden?' Although the youth only lived on top of the railway embankment close to where the Jews worked, he never saw the boy again and he blamed himself for not being observant and seeing the engineer approaching. This error of judgement cost him dearly in terms of that little extra food that could be the difference between life and death and he was indeed angry with himself.

In those relatively early days of the war with the Germans enjoying numerous crushing victories across Europe, a popular slogan appeared on virtually all Nazi lorries, buses and goods vehicles. It read, 'Alle Reder rolen vir den Sieg' which translated means 'all wheels are rolling for victory'. This was a great morale booster for Germany and its allies, but a particularly depressing picture for enemies of the Third Reich, especially the beleaguered Jewish race.

For a week or two at Lusenheim, Mayer was entrusted with the red flag for controlling traffic at level crossings. It was considered by many to be a cushy number but it paled somewhat in Mayer's mind when his Chief Engineer warned him that, if he caused any accident, he would pay with his life. The SS and Gestapo would approach in buses and would ignore his signals which obviously could lead to an accident. Mayer reported this to his engineer but he just shrugged his shoulders, clearly not in a frame of mind to remonstrate against the SS and the Gestapo. Numerous trains would be bringing materials of construction, it was a good job but had its attendant problems. He diced with death every day but nevertheless saved his strength over that one to two week period, a factor the importance of which could not be overstated with regard to survival.

Chapter Six

In Spring or early Summer 1942, with the job at Lusenheim completed, the surviving Jews, plus replacements, for there was seemingly a never ending source of replacements, were herded into cattle trucks once again for the approximately 25kms journey to camp number three at Guttenbrun, near Poznan.

Sometimes the foreman would move on with the labourers and sometimes not, but the Camp Commandant never ventured away from his allotted rail centre. The jobs at Guttenbrun were varied, starting with flattening mounds formed by the diggers, two men per mound, these jobs having to be finished on time or yet more beatings. He then moved on to unloading stone onto the railway track by digging from the top of a huge mountain of the material in a railway wagon. Three Jews worked to a wagon and to those who were last to empty their vehicle another sadistic beating ensued. It was a depressing task, back breaking in nature and certainly one that Mayer considered possibly one of the worst details. A job he much preferred was the unloading of horse manure with a fork, a warming task with significantly easier movement.

A team of German factory inspectors arrived and started asking many questions regarding the food supplied to the labouring Jews. 'Are you getting margarine? No! definitely not!' This and many other similar questions all received negative answers although they had to take care not to over exaggerate, for the foreman was always within earshot.

After they departed the standard of food improved with margarine and sugar making an appearance but it didn't last long. The inspectors concluded that the Jews had been in receipt of less than the regulation food ration, an obvious state of affairs of which all Jews were literally painfully aware. Jews could not complain however, they had no rights whatsoever, in effect they didn't really exist. For one or two days only after the visit, the prisoners received small amounts of sugar, no extra bread and no butter or margarine.

There were about 250 Jews at Guttenbrun and the only contact they had with civilians was when marching from the camp to work. The locals would spit at the Jews as they passed accompanied by verbal expletives, they had minds full of hatred, Jews were a nuisance to them and even the emaciated state of the labourers brought no compassion from the seething public.

"Mayer, do you think at the time if you had known how you were going to suffer in order to survive, would you have preferred not to have survived at all?"

"I've asked myself that question in hindsight many times and I honestly don't know. I suppose if I'd known how much I was going to suffer, I might well have considered finishing my life on the first day in the first camp. I do, however, come from a very religious Jewish family, a very sincere and a very honest family, to whom suicide is the worst crime of all because nothing is more precious than life itself. You must never give your life up and I am glad my upbringing taught me this, even if there was only the merest glimmer of hope. My thanks to my parents for they helped me get through the darkest days of my teenage years."

The prisoners could only gauge the ebb and flow of the

war by the expressions on the faces of the guards. Early on, elation, but later, as news worsened, distinctly more down in the mouth. Later on in January 1942 when injured German soldiers were coming back from the Eastern front with frostbite Mayer knew the Third Reich, with their heavy casualties, were going to lose the war and this made him more determined than ever to survive. His question at this stage to himself was, "are we going to see the end of the war?" They knew the Germans had frostbite because all the windows in the trains were fully open even in the depths of winter, a telltale clue to the terrible itching incurred in warmer temperatures from that most painful of frozen ailments. The trains were frequent and always full, sights that brought great joy within to the hapless Jews.

It was by now around the end of July 1943 and, even though surviving Jews remained buoyed by the sight of German causalities passing through from the Eastern front, hard labour was most exacting, in the heat of a Polish summer, to skeletal human beings whose strength was dwindling fast. Nevertheless Mayer's absence from Sieradz spared him the sights and sounds of the final elimination of his hometown's ghetto. Among those wretched hordes were his mother and three younger brothers.

The monastery in Mayer's hometown was considered an exalted place spiritually by the heavy presence of Catholics in the area and, one would imagine, above interference from the Nazi occupying forces. Not so it transpired, in fact nothing could be further from the truth. Not only did it become a collection centre for Jews to be transported to Chelmno and gassed en route, but, when America entered the war after Pearl Harbour, their American Sister was extracted from her holy duties and sent to the women's camp at Ravensbruck.

A nun's diary from the monastery in Sieradz provides a realistic picture of the conditions prevailing as Jews, in their thousands, waited for death by gassing van en route to Chelmno where the lifeless bodies were incinerated. It paints a picture of a helpless race, young and old, their acute fear and total humiliation. The diary entries are for week commencing Monday August 24th 1942, the very period when Mayer's mother and his three younger brothers were incarcerated in that same House of God.

Nun's Diary—Monastery at Sieradz
Monday 24th August 1942

Horrifying new events....uneasiness around the town. The Germans catch the Ghetto Jews and bring them to our church. The number of imprisoned Jewish families increases every hour. The Germans also bring in Zloczewos' Jews, as well from the surrounding area. They have already summoned around four thousand people at the church. Humming sounds like in a bee-hive, little children and adults sobbing.... The Germans do not allow anyone to leave the temple, not even to go out for their personal physiological needs.

Tuesday 25th August 1942

In the morning, along the church's arcades, we encounter a terrible smell, as well as streams of urine which flow under the doors. The nuns ran outside in order to bring sand to spread over the urine, they have collected it with spades and have loaded it on wheelbarrows clearing it away. They have piled sand in front of the church's doors and in front of the gate opposite the arcades. At about 10am, the police commandant's wife arrived bringing with her dirty underwear for the laundry. She asks for the meaning of the noise and the terrible smell. Paulina Jaskulanka, the nun, has answered: 'How come, you, the police commandant's wife does not know that in our church there are a few thousand Jews who are imprisoned and who are not even allowed to go out?'

Mrs Knocke answered: 'I really don't know anything because at home I talk to my husband only about office matters. But I will take care of it immediately.' And indeed, policemen came, they took five Jews with them to the station, gave them spades and ordered them to dig a hole in the garden by the church. They also asked them to pad the hole with wood. Since then they have allowed small groups of people to go out of the church. Although the Germans disliked it, the nuns have smuggled tea and milk for the infants as much as they could.

Amongst the imprisoned Jews, was Dr Kempinski, together with his wife. Some say that the Germans have offered him freedom, but this noble man and a great doctor had refused because he felt he was needed right there in such critical times.

As a result of the American bombers joining in the war against the Germans Hitler ordered to summon all American and British citizens residing in the occupied territories. One of our nuns, Sister Bernarda Mary Brennan, an Irish citizen, was also included among those detained. This afternoon, the police commandant had sent her, escorted by the police officer Meka, to our monastery. He confessed that although he was required to detain her in prison, since he trusted her not to escape, he would allow her to sleep at the monastery.

Wednesday 26th August 1942

Around 10 o'clock, tears in our eyes, we bid farewell to Sister Brennan who was to travel to an unknown destiny. Sister Miedzwiedzka has accompanied her, in a black carriage harnessed to a horse, to the station where she has found other people with foreign citizenship and who were at the same transport as Sister Brennan. The fact that she was not alone has calmed us down. The police officer escorting the transport said that the camp they were being sent to is located in Liebenau near Ravensburg.

The Germans have brought to the church another transport of Jews. It came to our attention that during the commotion an old man and boy were killed by one of the Germans, however, we could not verify whether there was any truth in this piece of information. No one heard the shootings. Although there has been unbearable overcrowding, the Jews have behaved with dignity in the church, deservedly for a holy place. During the evenings they were heard praying all together. Probably sensing what future lies ahead, occasionally, the Germans would pick a Jew from the church and escort him to his apartment. The Poles guessed the Germans knew about the economic situation of this or that merchant, and were hoping to find gold or jewellery, while promising to free them. Later on, they would return him back to the church. Nobody knew what was the purpose of all this, one can only guess.

It is necessary to mention here that prior to the final arrest of the Jews by the Germans, they used to torture them quite severely. Already in October 1939, under the command of A. Greiser, forced labour was ordered upon all the Jews between the ages of fourteen and sixty. Usually, they had to perform the most difficult physical jobs, where the food portions given to the Jews were the smallest. In 1941, Jews who were not 'employed', namely, the sick, the old and children, received weekly supplies of 100 gram corn-flour, 980 gram of whole wheat flour, 2.5 kg potatoes, 50 gram margarine, and a small amount of skimmed milk, per person. Working Jews received double portions. These Jews were guarded by German soldiers wearing black uniforms, who guarded them ruthlessly.

Friday 28th August 1942

It is most difficult to find the right words to describe the dreadful scenes that have appeared during the transportation of the Jews. Loads of Jewish women, old women and children, were loaded on a truck pushed towards the pavement in front of the monastery's gate. The men were grouped in threes in front of the church, choosing only those who were suitable for work. A terrible incident had occurred. A young man held on to his boy, refusing to give him up to the German who was trying to take him away. The Jew screamed: 'kill us both, but don't separate us!', he then was beaten with rifle butts until he fell over, he did not, however, let his son away from him. At the end, after a struggle with three police officers, he fell again and one of the torturers abducted the boy, throwing him on one of the trucks. The nuns who have seen the incident from the attic, heard one of the Germans at the scene of this diabolical incident, and who was usually employed at one of the monastery's offices, saying: 'and this is the German culture that people so speak about? I have to be ashamed to be a German!' Three days later this German, who was sensitive to the inhumanity to mankind, received his marching orders to the eastern front. Fellow countrymen revealed his views and opinions. Most of the Jews have found their death in the Chelmno area, by the River Ner. Trucks came and left several times, carrying Jewish citizens of our town and of the surrounding area to a terrible and definite death.

Saturday 29th August 1942

Just before noon, the remaining Jews at the church were taken away. This time they were the young men destined for work. Immediately after permission was received from the Germans and the nuns started to clean up the church. Whoever was available, stood by with spades, brooms and dusters. Such a massive gathering of human beings, with no permission granted for them to 'go out' from the very first day, has caused immense pollution, even though the Jews have tried partially to take care of the cleaning. The nuns have scraped the floors and the altars. Although it was a joint effort it took them half a day to complete the cleanings. After two days of ventilating the church we have continued on Monday as well.

Sunday 30th August 1942

Massive marching to the holy Mass in Charlupa, in order to ask God to take under his wings the sacrifice of blood of the innocent Jews. Despite our sincere and strong desire we could only help them very little. Since the parents wouldn't separate from their children we couldn't save even one single child. The parents were frightened, so frightened even of their own shadow. A long time afterwards, while walking along the arcades, we could feel and hear the humming and the longing songs sung by the Jews imprisoned in our church.

Several points of interest can be gleaned from the nun's

diary, some confirmatory in nature and others, considering background religious issues, somewhat surprising. For the Nazis to show utter contempt to the native race of the country they occupied was no surprise and, in this instance, the selection of the monastery for their most horrendous selection process personified their total lack of consideration in this stronghold of Catholicism. To further rub salt in the wound the treatment of children and the elderly of the Jewish faith as though they were animals, thereby rendering the monastery in effect an open toilet, further reflected the arrogance of the Germans. On the other hand, proof that not every German condoned the scandalous treatment of Jews also emerged from the pages of the diary. Given the marked anti-Semitic feelings of Polish Catholics both before, during, and after the war, the compassion and sympathy shown by the nuns to the Jews was to be admired and applauded. By smuggling in tea and milk for the Jews they took great risks indeed in trying to help their fellow human beings, irrespective of their religion. The nuns were seriously impressed with the dignity shown by the Jews in such adversity and truly appreciated that fact within their own most spiritual walls.

The elder Jews usually knew the Jewish calendar better than the young ones but people who knew that calendar as well as anybody were the Germans and they usually arranged their worst atrocities to happen on special Jewish holidays, whether in towns or camps. In towns the Nazis would go on shooting sprees, murdering people and enjoying wanton destruction of Jewish property. In camps it would be public hangings and beatings, the latter being so ferocious that many died from them. In all these reprisals all the inmates would be made to watch and, if any spectators turned their gaze away from the humiliations, they'd be shot instantly.

The camp at Guttenbrun, like the two previous railway camps, was not enclosed by fencing and therefore escape was theoretically possible. The totally exhausted condition of the prisoners meant few considered chancing such a risky proposition and those who did were shot and their limp bodies leant against their shovels for all to see. And the Germans made sure that all their former colleagues had a long look at the futile attempts at escape from enslavement. Even though most spirits by now had been well and truly broken, the Nazis never missed an opportunity of pressing the message home and revelling in the pleasure the measures brought. As in his first two camps, Guttenbrun whittled the number of prisoners down periodically when new arrivals would allow by a somewhat theatrical selection process. The Jews were never undressed to facilitate a meaningful medical examination and the Germans would decide how many to exterminate that particular day by a mere glance, nothing more. If the selector took a dislike to you then your ticket was booked on the gassing van standing only yards away from the selection group. The victims knew where they were going one hundred per cent and the resulting brutal measures used to force them into the van were physically sickening to the watching survivors. Clubs and whips were used excessively, the dismissed group of humanity bloodied beyond recognition, their cries and screams to no avail except only to further torment the crazed minds of the onlookers.

One night at his third camp Mayer had great need to relieve himself, it was after nine o'clock and he knew it was strictly forbidden to leave one's barrack at that time. In deep snow, barefooted, he took a chance, managing to come back in one piece. The barrack was in total darkness when he was unfortunate to catch his left knee against the corner of a bunk bed, this injury turning into an open wound. This camp boasted a so called hospital, Lanzerett the Germans called it, there was no medication but, what was worse, it was purely an assembly point for the gassing van. Every so often the gassing van would arrive and empty the hospital of its content of patients. He had no intention of volunteering for an early end to his life and so, with great perseverance he marched to work, jumping on one leg. One fine day Mayer, asked his foreman whether he could work in the camp itself for there was always plenty of maintenance work to be done there and this would enable him to avoid the march to and from the work place. His request was approved but one afternoon he could see the gassing van arriving, the whistle blew and an announcement declared that everyone was to come to roll call. He knew if he did so he would be dead in about 15 to 20 minutes. He did not move as the SS man, with a gun in his hand, approached his barrack shouting and screaming that if any man found hiding did not come out there and then, that man would be shot. "What difference does it make if you die from a bullet or die in the gassing van," Mayer's thought turned over in his mind as he noticed that a rear window was open. Hard labour slaves were indeed fortunate to have a window at all, let alone one that opened and, when the guard was close, Mayer, with his heart beating like a drum, jumped out of the back window and, when he heard him coming to the back of the barracks, he jumped back in again. The SS guard was satisfied that everyone

the foreman intervened saying that he was young but also a good worker. Although this foreman saved Mayer's life he was nevertheless a brute of a man who, if he took a dislike to a person, would beat that person so vehemently he would kill him. As the work was completed at Guttenbrun in May 1943 survivors were sent off, Mayer to his fourth location, and that most infamous of death camps, Auschwitz-Birkenau. The German name meant nothing to him, nor had he ever heard of it from any other Jew. For all he knew it was going to be a fourth railway camp. Non Jews of every conceivable nationality knew of its existence and its purpose, for they drove the trains there and they witnessed the brutal forcing of victims into those stinking cattle trucks at the point of departure. The concentration camp was given the German name Auschwitz, to be known in Poland as the 'Death Camp', and was situated near the Polish town of Oswiecim on marshy ground between the Vistula and its tributary, the River Sola. The camp originated in 1940, its nucleus consisting of old garrison barracks and disused factory premises and was located near the road which ran along the Sola river, connecting Auschwitz with the village of Rajsko.

Chapter Seven

Mayer had already survived three years and two months of slave labour prior to arrival at Birkenau and in that time he often thought if the Germans' treatment of Jews useful to the Third Reich was so sadistically cruel, then how do they treat Jews back home who do not offer this industrial advantage? All three railway construction camps had been extremely brutal and deaths by beatings, starvation, suicide and selection would be relatively equally split between the three. After careful consideration though he picked Otoczno as the most barbaric, no doubt coming straight from home to his first slave labour camp had made a damning impression on his young mind.

The trip from Guttenbrun took about two days travelling day and night in crowded cattle trucks with neither food nor water, approximately ninety prisoners per truck, with merely a bucket as a toilet. Again the demoralising screaming of the guards urging the Jews on with club and whip and Mayer wondered why this was still necessary, for his people's spirit was already well broken. In reality he believed the Nazis enjoyed seeing the fear in Jewish eyes. They were transferred to the shower room where they were all examined naked for any hidden valuables.

They gave up all their clothing and were tattooed on the arm with a number, Mayer's being 138528. From that point onwards their names were completely disregarded, they were no longer human beings, merely a number. Their camp uniform issue consisted of striped jacket, trousers, cap, shirt, underpants and ill-fitting shoes. Even though the Polish winters were extremely cold they had no winter clothing such as pullovers, overcoats or warmer underwear. Most of the time they worked out of doors and had to stand in the open twice a day for roll call in all kinds of weather, hot summer sunshine, rain, snow and always freezing winter temperatures down to minus twenty two degrees. The Nazis were making it an impossible struggle for these human skeletons against the cruel elements.

The new arrivals were put initially in quarantine camp for a couple of weeks, the block leader in charge of Mayer's barrack being a bow legged Jewish criminal, who was a good actor with a loud voice and could speak German and Polish, although his language would shock good living people.

After the quarantine period Mayer's new home in Birkenau, and for his entire eighteen month stay, was barrack 24 in D camp, built originally to house 52 horses, with tethering rings still in position, it had three tier bunk beds and, when full, held one thousand men. He remembered the SS barracks not far from the entrance to Birkenau, the Jewish A camp being closest to the foreboding railway arch and subsequent letters of the alphabet running back in the direction of the even more foreboding crematoria. In charge of the barrack was the block leader, a German Jew who had been a long serving prisoner in Buchenwald from 1938. He was a refined man who, as a political prisoner, had been brutalised, although his only crime was to be a Jew. He bore a red triangle on his striped uniform to signify a political prisoner. Jews had a yellow triangle, black for Jehovah's Witnesses, pink for homosexuals, whilst a green triangle denoted a criminal. Under him was the barrack secretary, a non Jewish Pole who dealt with paperwork and kept the records up to date. Mayer wasn't sure if he was there at the beginning but he was still present when Mayer moved to his next camp. The secretary had a stiff bearing and was somewhat aloof, he was a cruel and hard man but clever for, with an eye to survival post war, he learned English from a Polish Jew. The third in the pecking order were the three stubendiensts or room orderlies and these five were in privileged positions for they had total food control in the barrack and therefore always looked healthier. The Germans were not bothered how the food was shared out, an attitude of mind that put great power in the hands of the three officer levels in each barrack, especially the block leader.

Also in 24D was Fritz, a German criminal who was good-humoured although forever using bad language. He escaped from his place of work and went to a pub for a drink, but was recaptured and brought back. His head was shaven and he wore the same stripes as all prisoners, although that is where the similarities ended. Despite escaping he was not executed and he would never go through the selection process. A French Jew and fellow inmate of 24D was sometimes Mayer's Kapo, especially later when both worked on the construction of the 'Mexico' camp and he shouted and acted tough with the best of them, he had to for his job was on the line if he didn't. Nevertheless he was a good guy and certainly not to be confused with some Kapos who were as sadistic as the SS. Another member of 24D was a Jewish foreman from Zdunska Wola by the name of Katz, a man who was fair and reasonable and whom Mayer was to ask not to beat his brother, Yakov, when the latter arrived at Auschwitz some months later. The Kapo's position brought with it a slightly more generous food ration but not to compare with that of the block leader and his four cohorts with total power over food allocation. It might be assumed that a block leader would be able to see the war out with his more plentiful supply of food, but that assumption does not stand up because of the favourite German pastime of playing games with Jewish lives. In German eyes these sub humans were to be used, brutalised and finally destroyed. Block leaders, secretaries, whatever their position, would one day have their card marked and they would be issued forth from one of the four crematoria chimneys. Mayer had at least three block leaders in what was going to be his eighteen month stint at Auschwitz Birkenau. His block leader in 24D was a German Jew and, from the way he spoke, it was obvious he was a well-educated man who came from an intellectual family. Although he had first choice of the food in the barrack, the leader was nevertheless expected by the Germans to be absolutely tough and ruthless with his charges, exercising total discipline over them. Eventually he was taken away and never seen again, maybe not sufficiently brutal, prisoners could only conjecture the point. He was a mere pawn in the German's game of life and death, and once again confirmed the position of block leader was anything but permanent. The vacancy was then filled by a tall slim non Jewish Pole, a nice, well-spoken chap who was to retain the position for the rest of Mayer's stay there. All in all his three block leaders were reasonably fair to their subordinates.

Their quarantine block leader, the short, bow legged man, had been a prisoner pre-war at the Sieradz gaol and David Josefowicz's father was in at the same time for a minor offence. His dad knew the local farmers and was able to obtain food which he shared with this block leader, a fact that would play an important part in David's time at Birkenau. It was a case of divine providence, for David's father was only in prison because he kept geese and, by that time, German law banned Jews from keeping livestock. Nevertheless, after returning home, he continued to keep geese, clearly making a statement that he, like his son, was prepared to take risks in order to survive. David, who worked in the kinder block and was ready to be taken to the gas chambers, always took chances and ran away into the latrines up to his neck in excrement. Under cover of darkness David made his way to a barrack, any barrack, and good fortune smiled on him. David pleaded with the block leader to let him stay but he refused because all his charges were accounted for. 'Who are you anyway?', the man in charge snapped, 'I'm David Josefowicz from Sieradz', came the apprehensive reply. The block leader's eyes suddenly opened fully. 'Your father's name?',

'Henoch', David stammered nervously. 'Any son of Henoch Josefowicz is welcome here'. David was not only saved but, in being accepted into that particular barrack, had the good fortune to have, in his company, a group of non Jewish Poles, including some from Sieradz. Being Christians, these people received letters and food parcels from home and David was the fortunate recipient of some precious extra food and news of how the war was progressing. Jews were not only starved of food but also of information from the worldwide war fronts.

David told Mayer of a true story originating from the kinder block, another of the many situations in this hell-hole where fate ruled between life and death. It was Simchat Tora, the most joyful day in the Jewish calendar, the day that celebrated the conclusion of the reading of the Holy Scrolls. Consequently the children were singing joyous songs appropriate to the festival, assembled as they were in readiness to be gassed. The SS guard outside was very annoyed at all the vocal renderings and he opened the door and enquired of one of the boys, "why are you so jubilant?". The lad replied confidently and without any hesitation, "because today is Simchat Tora, the rejoicing of the law, and soon we will be dead and go to heaven and our suffering in this hell will be over!" The SS man dragged this boy out of the barrack, snarling as he did so, "no, you are not going with the rest." This boy of eleven years of age was the only survivor of the war in that entire building.

Remembering there were no women in the Jewish male areas, Mayer personally didn't come across any homosexual activity and the only people he knew who cared for sexual gratification were the block leader and his four officers. These five had clout when it came to bargaining, for their surplus food enabled them to obtain young boys, known as pupils, for sexual enactment. For the merest scrap of bread the pupils would dance to their master's tune, the Germans turning a blind eye to this behaviour.

There was only one Auschwitz Birkenau, it was top of the league table for indescribable conditions, for the scale of human elimination accomplished, for the level of depravation of Jews and generally the greatest example of man's inhumanity to man. Jews were there from all over Europe and Mayer remembers Greek port workers from Salonica, strong and tough, they were an obvious target, a challenge as it were to SS brutalities. They soon disappeared and it was rumoured that they were transferred to the Sonderkommandos who needed to be strong for dealing with multitudes of corpses in the gas chambers and crematoria. They were better fed but their term of work was four months and then elimination, in order that the outside world remain ignorant of the scale of the Holocaust, for these people saw everything there was to be seen when it came to the super efficient method of extermination of an entire race. It has often been reported over the years that conditions in the cattle trucks were so appalling that words were totally inadequate in painting a picture of the squalor and misery of the total dehumanisation of one race by others. The picture could be imagined to show a significantly more inhumane image when those inmates were made to wait several hours before the doors were slid open in winter temperatures down to minus 22 degrees or, alternatively summer heat of possibly 30 degrees. These contrasting climatic conditions amid the heavy stench of excrement in wagons awash with urine are difficult to comprehend and appreciate by those only used to a normal hygienic atmosphere. Mayer witnessed the arrival of many such trainloads in wagons dripping urine and shared with others the shocking experience of listening to the piercing screams of the victims fighting for air and the lower pitched moans from many who had little will to live left. Such strains were sweet music to the ears of the hard-line Nazis. A train arriving in the evening would be left overnight prior to the selection process, lest the process interfere with, perhaps, a Dr Mengele cocktail party or some equally interesting subject matter arising from yet another inhumane experimentation programme. Capable of understanding German, Mayer could hear the guards scream at the victims to leave all their hand luggage on the platform and wave the old and infirm to a waiting cart, not for any humane consideration, simply to expedite more efficiently this human dross, in German eyes, off the face of the planet. Many mercifully had passed away on what for multitudes were long journeys of four days and more. Jewish prisoners were on the platform moving the newcomers along and helping the elderly get down from the train. These prisoners were comparatively strong and because he was not all that strong, Mayer never worked on this detail and for this he was grateful, because mixing with these innocent people, looking as they did in their torment even more hapless, would have brought back memories of his parents, bringing more emotional trauma.

The levels of torment produced, at every turn, by Auschwitz were so intense that the length of time individuals could withstand this pressure varied greatly, suicide being the ultimate choice of many. Mayer remembered several times when leaving the barrack early in the morning the sight of those inmates, who had decided to end it all the previous day, still clinging to the wire whilst nearby the German warning pronounced, 'hochstnung lebensgefahr!', 'high voltage danger', the last word conveyed by the image of a skull. He witnessed prisoners walking into the wire when death would be accomplished in seconds but, if the guards saw them, they would shoot them in order to save having to switch off the current prior to taking the body down. Nothing succeeded more in increasing the depth of total despair on the Jews than the sight of their former colleagues hanging limply from a gallows, or rigidly held to the wire as if by a magnet. In the Jewish faith life itself was sacred, God gave life and only God should take it away and thus suicide is consequently frowned upon. Mayer, however, would be the first to admit that Auschwitz constituted extenuating circumstances.

Jews were always an expendable commodity at Auschwitz and, regardless of how many a German foreman lost through disease, it mattered little, for there were millions more to take their places. The food available to the Jews was not intended to keep them there for long. They would be given a minimal ration of mouldy bread made from wild chestnuts and sprinkled with sawdust, whilst some 'enjoyed', if that's the word, a kind of margarine, whose basic ingredient was lignite, a low grade brownish-black coal; thirty grams of sausage made from the flesh of mangy horses made up the entire offering which was not to exceed 700 calories. To wash this ration down, a half litre of soup made from nettles and weeds, containing nothing fatty, no flour, no salt. Thousands of families arrived daily and any visibly pregnant women were sent immediately to the gas chambers. It was total madness but the murderers were not madmen.

By now his previous three camps, which, at the time he had thought were hell on earth, seemed, suddenly, to be quite reasonable establishments. That was the effect Auschwitz had on the tormented mind of a Jew. This man-made centre of genocide had to be worse than hell, for he could not see anyone anywhere improving on the techniques of torment honed by the Nazis for the elimination of an entire race. He had befriended a nineteen year old who suddenly one day was taken away for medical experimentation. The boy came back, having received no anaesthetic, with only one testicle. There was also a set of twins in barrack 24D, Polish Jews, who were one day taken out on an experimentation programme, one returning badly mutilated, and the other was never seen again. The surviving twin, although never in the best of health, lived through the

Mayer's father, Isaac Lajb Herszkowicz circa 1919. He
died in the gas chambers at Auschwitz during August 1944.

Mayer's sister, Kajla, who died in January 1945 by drowning when, with a thousand other women, she was put aboard a ship subsequently scuttled in ice cold Baltic waters.

A German photograph of Mr Kliszczenko, a glazier by trade,. This very poor Jew with ten children was a very happy man, always singing. This picture was taken just before the Germans secured him to the tallest building in Sieradz, telling him to carry on singing. It was January 1940. They left him there and he died of hypothermia, The picture shows him smiling, a prerequisite the Germans insisted upon for all their photographs.

A German photograph of a Rabbi and his son in the ghetto of Warta, circa 1939, immediately before the son hung his father on the order of the Nazis. The Rabbi gave his son permission to do this because of the German promise to let the boy live. Moments after the hanging the boy was shot.

A German photograph of Mr Apertit with the chief of the SS, Mr Bleim, pictured together in the ghetto of Sieradz in about 1940. Bleim obviously revelled in his licence to brutalise, for, long after the war had ended, in the 1980s, Polish compatriots with long memories located him living prosperously in Germany. In mysterious circumstances Bleim and his wife died when their bungalow caught fire.

German photograph showing the deportation of women from the Sieradz ghetto to Chelmno in 1941/42.
The lady in the foreground was, strangely, the only survivor of this group.

Photograph taken by a Czech partisan showing, on May 8th 1945, the arrival of an open coal waggon at Theresienstadt after a three week journey from Buchenwald. Initially this waggon would have held 100 Jews, with the dead being removed and buried periodically as the journey progressed, for the Germans were most particular in hiding evidence of the greatest crime in world history. These prisoners had neither food nor water during the three week journey.

Some of the children gathered together by the Jewish committee in Prague on August 14th 1945 immediately prior to their flight to Carlisle, England and a new life. Mayer is in the middle row, fifth from the right.

In Tel Aviv, April 1990. Left to right, Mayer, his elder brother Yakov, his uncle Maurice and Judith, Mayer's wife.

A copy of page 194 of the admissions book at Theresienstadt showing Meier Herschkowitx coming from Scheratz (German spelling) and being born on June 8th 1929 instead of his true birthday, August 31st 1926. The reasons for this deception was because young Jews had to be under eighteen to be accepted to enter England. Earlier, for survival in the camps, he had to be shown as older than his real age.

David Josefowicz working in a kibbutz in Losau in Germany in 1945. This farm work was in preparation for his impending illegal emigration to Israel.

A German soldier ordering Famusz Kon to run prior to threatening to shoot him in the back. They fired several times, deliberately just missing the boy, who experienced a nerve racking ordeal. His parents owned the ironmongery shop in Castle Street. Although humiliated he somehow managed to survive this moment of German sport, and then the camps, eventually to emigrate and live in Canada.

David Josefowicz's father, Henoch, in the black hat, being thrown out of his home in Castle Street during the process of running down the Sieradz ghetto.

After the formation of the ghettos, non-Jews were not allowed to trade with the Jews. In this German photograph taken in the ghetto of Zdunska Wola, the non-Jewish customer on the left and his Jewish tailor were both publically hanged immediately after this picture was taken.

A German soldier with a Jew pictured in the market place in Sieradz during the early days of occupation when Jews could still trade there. Since they could no longer travel they were unable to find their full range of goods. This picture would be sent home to Germany to show the difference between the master race and the sub-humans. And of course the Jew had to smile.

Wanda Turowiczowa, the owner of the pharmacy in Sieradz and a non-Jew, with a selection of the extra set of German prints carefully saved for posterity by Henryka Szturme, the non-Jewish photographic processor.

Mayer's Marathon of Misery

Date	From	To	Distance (miles)
March 1940	Home in Sieradz	Otoczno	75
Spring 1941	Otoczno	Lusenheim	20
Spring 1942	Lusenheim	Guttenbrun	20
May 1943	Guttenbrun	Auschwitz	200
November 1944	Auschwitz	Stutthoff	300
December 1944	Stutthof	Stuttgart	600
February 1945	Stuttgart	Gotha	180
April 1st 1945	Gotha	Buchenwald	50
April 8th 1945	Buchenwald	Theresienstadt	200

He was liberated on May 8th 1945.
He weighed just four stone.

war and eventually emigrated to New York. After the war this single twin advertised in the Jewish Telegraph for any surviving twins who had been incarcerated in Auschwitz, mentioning that his barrack was 24D. Mayer promptly replied stating that he remembered the twins in that hut and later received a most welcome reply from the man whose forenames were Hersh Mayer!

Mengele was a medical doctor, theoretically a man brought up to save lives, but at Auschwitz he revelled in human experimentation, perhaps the bottom of this pit of evil hadn't yet been reached.

Mayer was gaining experience on how to survive, the main quality required was never to appear ill and always look reasonably fit. For instance, if a Jew had skin disease and a rash promoting the need to itch, he was immediately a potential victim in the selection process. If he was seen scratching he would be a certainty for the gas chambers.

There was a time when he had a severe abscess on his back, if left it could send him up in smoke. He decided to have it removed under full anaesthetic, knowing full well that, unless he was out of the hospital quickly, he risked being sent to the gas chambers. To linger in hospital invited a visit to the final solution.

Mayer learnt many tricks including hiding under the lower bunk and sometimes another Jew would want to hide under the same lower bunk. This was a crazy idea and he would persuade him to try somewhere else. A German guard would enter the barrack after all had left and bluff a Jew out of a hiding place simply by saying, 'come out I can see you'. Those who fell for it were never seen again.

Toilet facilities consisted simply of two wooden barrels and every morning the block leader or room orderly would quickly select four inmates to empty these two heavy containers into the latrines outside. This they did by supporting the barrels on two wooden poles, it was a terrible job with obnoxious spillages enforced by the heavy weight involved. Mayer was never selected for this detail because he guessed that he did not look sufficiently strong, which was fortunate indeed, for the indiscriminate selection process could have led to him dropping his corner and putting himself at risk in the survival stakes. In daytime the barrack would be empty save for the block leader, the secretary and those prisoners who were too sick to work. Instead they would clean the barrack and scrub the concrete floor. All Jews had to be present for roll call but, after that arduous exercise had been completed, the Kapos would select their men for their particular work party that day. It was during this selection that Mayer would sometimes hide under the bottom bunk in order to escape work and avoid an up to two hour march to and from the site. He managed to achieve this risky deception only two or three times but these were contributory factors to his survival, for the energy savings accrued were absolutely vital to those so nearly dead on their feet.

Auschwitz was hell on earth, a terrible torment day and night. They would march out to work in the morning past the Jewish orchestra, including many of Europe's greatest musicians, and if anyone was out of step they were beaten sadistically. If the same thing happened returning to the camp at night, the offending Jew's number was taken and he would be in the next selection. Another rule for survival therefore was obey the rules, even down to marching in step.

On arrival at Auschwitz-Birkenau, Mayer was one of

only a few survivors from the previous camps and the first thing they were all to lose instantly was their very identity for they each had a six figure number etched onto their arm. Their individual names were discarded. They were then all issued with camp clothing, before being marched into their barrack to join others already there. The block leader, who was himself a prisoner, called them to follow him; he said, "listen you lads, do you think Auschwitz is a holiday camp? I can assure you not, nobody survives here, in fact you will all go through those chimneys over there." With this happy thought they were all allocated different bunk beds. They had three layers and you were fortunate indeed if you were young and agile enough to reach the top shelf because this position had certain advantages. Those men occupying the lower levels had to suffer the most terrible indignities with all kinds of rubbish falling onto them due to many inmates suffering from all types of diseases, diarrhoea, rubbish from dirty boots, everything obeyed the laws of gravity. They had no mattresses just hard boards and the inmates were all skin and bone. Come night time one would think, being so exhausted, sleep would be possible even in these primitive conditions. One would be wrong however, for the nocturnal hours were saved for body shaving and head shaving and also painting the body with a disinfectant solution. If that was not enough, the guards would complain that the slaves reaction time to the early morning whistle was too slow and insisted on the Jews perfecting this fast timing. Through the night they would continually rehearse the procedure and, since the population of the huts was continually changing due to the high death rate, this gross interruption to sleep went on indefinitely.

Again in the morning they would have to rise at half past three and soon afterwards were allowed to go to the big latrine and then guards were standing outside with whips forcing them in and more guards inside with whips persuading them to leave just as quickly. Their toilet was the ultimate in primitiveness, merely a fairly narrow length of wood across a large pit, and should any prisoners not get their balance just right, so they would fall into the muck and that was literally the end of them. Although Mayer did not witness such a happening personally, other colleagues of his did see prisoners stripped of the strength to save themselves, consequently drowning in the faecal matter. This did constitute another avenue for suicide, but there were more cleaner and quicker routes for those who could take no more. There were times, every so often, that they were allowed to go and be deloused which entailed being taken to a large shower room, forced to get undressed and throw their clothing into the steaming trap and their underpants into disinfectant solution, believed to be calcium chloride, a substance also used to wash the head after shaving, a drop of which could burn the eyes quite badly. The guards were standing with horse whips on the edge of the shower room beating the prisoners and screaming at them to get into the icy cold water. No soap, no towels and when wringing wet they had to get out and run back to their barracks and put on their underpants still dripping wet from the disinfectant. Many contracted pneumonia and died and it was only in the barrack that you would receive your clothing back.

Some mornings, after roll call, an announcement would be made that the Jews would not go to work that day, for they were always a mixed gang of prisoners there, incorporating all kinds of nationalities. Jews knew of course what it meant. They would be forced into the barrack, get undressed in very cold Polish winters without any heating and they would have to wait for Dr Mengele to come along and select his victims who were going to die that day. Mengele was a shortish man, always immaculately dressed and very confident in himself, who always seemed totally disinterested in the selection process, so vital to those bent on survival. Being a big camp they would sometimes have to wait a long time for him or Dr Johann Kremer or one of the other doctors to arrive eventually. So numerous were they Mayer cannot put an accurate figure on the number of times he survived Mengele's life or death selection process. Fortunately for Mayer the decision was always that he should live another day. Most of the selections, but not all, were performed when the prisoners were naked, those chosen to die did not have their clothes returned to them, their numbers were written down and their file taken from the records. Mengele or his assistant would know that morning exactly how many he needed to be killed that day, bearing in mind the number of newly arriving prisoners expected, in order to keep the crematoria working to full capacity.

On one occasion a colleague of Mayer's, who was the same age, felt very sorry for himself when he was selected to die, for when the victim was so chosen he was not allowed to put his clothes on again. Addressing Mayer, the young boy said indignantly, "Why was I picked? I look no worse than you." A couple nearby, in an attempt to comfort the lad with the only truth that they knew, said, "your suffering has finished now, ours will go on a bit longer and we will die just the same." He went in the usual style of an open lorry containing naked bodies and when it arrived at the gas chambers it was tipped just like it would tip a lorry load of soil. In fact many times as they were marching to and from work they could see these same lorries with women prisoners also being taken to the gas chambers. They could hear them crying but they did not know whether they were crying because of the fate that was awaiting them or the discomfort and cold that they felt. They did not know whether to feel pity for them or envy but there was simply nothing they could do to make their ordeal any better.

Those Jews who were propelled by Dr Mengele's left thumb were rendered by the gas chambers into a corpse often within an hour of their arrival at Auschwitz. Not so fortunate were those who were directed by the same infamous Doctor into the right hand column. He remained a candidate for death, but with this significant difference, that for three or four months, or as long as he could endure, he had to submit to all the horrors that Auschwitz had to offer, until he dropped from utter exhaustion. He felt pain from multitudes of beatings, his stomach was contorted with hunger, his eyes haggard and he moaned like a person demented. He dragged his tormented body across the fields of snow till he could go no further. At this stage more beatings would fail to move him, for his hour of deliverance, the hour of his redeeming death was close at hand. Of the millions of Jews who perished at Auschwitz, who were more fortunate? Those who went to the left or those who went to the right? Mayer went to the right on no less than forty occasions in the eighteen months he spent at Auschwitz-Birkenau after selections by Dr Mengele or his assistant. Mayer was certainly fortunate indeed, for extremely few could match his length of time in survival mode. To sum up the dire lot of the Jew at Auschwitz, it has to be said that Jews and non-Jews were treated similarly with respect to brutalities, the great difference was that only Jews were put through the agonising trauma of the life or death selections. Also Jews were given less food than anyone else, a minimal quantity to enable the extraction of some work contribution to the Third Reich cause, but always to ultimately feed the insatiable needs of the four Birkenau crematoria.

"Imagining the starkly dramatic images of the four crematoria belching out smoke and flame, it would be difficult indeed to imagine you never experienced flashbacks or nightmares?" I suggested.

"Yes, I certainly suffer from lifelike memories of those irrepressible pictures of horror. Only the other night I dreamt about some colleagues of mine who died in the Holocaust. Someone's voice came through so clearly and distinctly, "we have to go to the dentist to get the gold teeth out." I woke up trembling, beads of sweat crowding my brow. Auschwitz never lets you escape, not even fifty eight years later."

It was an amazing fact that, such was the scale of the extermination of Jews and other undesirables, no less than thirty five barracks in Birkenau never housed a prisoner throughout the war. These huts were known as 'Canada', a country believed to be of great wealth by the locals, some relatives of whom had emigrated just before the war and almost immediately were in a position to send money home. These buildings stored the loot literally stripped from millions of prisoners. To further appreciate the vast scale of this pilfering from innocents, on January 23rd 1945, four days before the liberation of the camp by the Soviet army, SS men set fire to thirty of these barracks filled with the property seized from murdered people. The buildings burnt for several days. In six partly burnt barracks the following objects were found after liberation. 1,185,345 men's suits and women's clothes, 43,255 pairs of men's and women's shoes, 13,694 carpets and great quantities of brushes, shaving brushes and other articles of daily use. After the war many people might have wondered how it came about that the SS who, at the beginning of the conflict, were hardly able to afford the equipment they needed, a few years later were in a position to buy out whole streets with impressive administration buildings. Corruption and immorality were common place amongst Hitler's elite and, even though punishments to their own were extremely severe, it continued and associated black marketeers made huge profits.

The group of barracks given the collective name of Canada was a source of great wealth to the Third Reich, each building housing a particular commodity, be it spectacles, shoes and boots, all types of brushes, human hair, gold, jewellery and all types of luggage. Word among the inmates suggested working in Canada was a relatively easy assignment when measured on the Auschwitz scale of horror. Mayer was never placed in the position of confirming or denying this generally accepted opinion. The temptation to steal from such an establishment was a permanent dare to those who worked in sorting this neverending treasure trove, designed to continually fill the coffers in Berlin. The Germans occasionally searched the Canada labourers quite unexpectedly and, any found with something they shouldn't have were publicly flogged and then, equally publicly hanged. All prisoners were forced to watch these public spectacles to act as a warning. Mayer knew one man who worked there and one day this man tempted the young prisoner from Sieradz to help change a one hundred dollar note into lower denominations. He went completely against his naturally cautious character by agreeing to smuggle the note out in the heel of his boot from his place of work back to barrack 24D. The Germans would often resort to random checks when they might ask the prisoners to remove their shoes. It was an insanely crazy risk to take but food was short and he needed more to cheat the selection process. As luck had it the note escaped detection and, in the short time available to him after roll call, and the miserly food rations, to curfew, he passed it to a man. In the evening after work, in a lower numbered barrack in D camp, this person was to change it to smaller bills, minus his commission of course. Next night Mayer went to collect the lower denomination notes, only to be told by his contact that the man to whom he had given it, had lost the one hundred dollar bill. "Was he lying?", he mused, one could never tell, the only thing he knew for sure was neither he nor the originator of the mission could go to the authorities! An incredible risk taken in this instance had failed to produce that vital extra food but, at least, lady luck had saved his hide again to survive another day.

In Auschwitz there was no hope whatsoever, there was total and utter despair. In fact many times in the morning they could see people committing suicide, for all they had to do was walk up to the double barbed wire fence which was electrified, with six thousand volts of current passing through it, and they would be electrocuted. It was a quick, clean release from life's unbearable torments. Sometimes the guard would notice them before touching the wire and he would shoot them. Mayer saw many walk to the fence in total despair, this action being characteristic of numerous intellectuals who clearly could see no hope and could not stand the anguish. He was only yards away from many who committed suicide and, in his experience, they all went quietly to the wire with no shouting or cursing. The Germans were so organised and methodical with each section of fence having its own switch for the removal of the dead, whilst leaving the remainder of the perimeter wire live.

The work was varied, sometimes Mayer worked in the camp itself building improvised drainage systems, repairing roads, and sometimes outside Auschwitz-Birkenau building a new camp which was called 'Mexico' and assembling barracks therein. As late as 1943 this new camp was intended for British people but luckily Hitler and Himmler never succeeded in achieving this goal. This 'Mexico' camp was a comparatively short march from the entrance to Birkenau and Mayer worked there for months rather than weeks and, although it was hard work unloading the wooden stock from trains and erecting the barracks, he found this time more reasonable than most due mainly to knowing Katz, the foreman from Zdunska Wola and the French Jew Kapo from barrack 24D. These two expected you to work but were fair, nevertheless screaming and cursing their team in the presence of the SS. Some days were long for, should a train arrive late in the day, the prisoners would have to off load it before returning to Birkenau, ensuring that even the sizeable orchestra, numbering possibly twenty five of the cream of European instrumentalists, was kept waiting to play them in through that threatening arch. The comparative absence of beatings on this job was an important factor, for they sapped one's strength rapidly and, should a Kapo or foreman pick on you for no reason at all, your days were numbered. Parts of Mexico were used for the Hungarian Jews, such was the torrent of numbers of these doomed people descending on Auschwitz-Birkenau in 1944, the result of that arch demon, Adolf Eichmann, putting his foot on the gas pedal for Jewish elimination with chances of a victory for the Third Reich then slipping away.

"It is often reported that some Jewish Kapos were more brutal than the SS. Did you experience this? And, if so, wouldn't this lead to conflict back in the barrack between Kapos and the men?"

"In my experience that statement is incorrect, for the Ukrainian SS were, in most cases, significantly more cruel than the German SS. Again speaking from experience, the Jewish Kapos made a lot of noise, it was expected of them by the Germans, but, generally speaking it was verbal rather than blows that rained down from Jew to Jew. Indeed this was mainly the position due to Kapo and slave labourer sharing the same barrack."

There were occasions whilst working on this new camp when delays were encountered and the party would be late returning to Birkenau. This being the case, the orchestra would be made to wait in often freezing conditions in order to play the work party in. If any one single person was not there, the rest of the prisoners would be forced to stand for hours at a time in all weathers until the missing prisoner was found. He was either shot or beaten to death on capture with his body being brought back on display for them all to see. At other times when the missing prisoner was discovered, he was brought alive to camp and then hanged with all the prisoners being forced to walk around and observe that painful spectacle. Even the guards were not allowed off duty until the person was found, dead or alive.

During June and July 1944 thousands of postcards were given out to the inmates of overcrowded barracks, in particular new arrivals, with instructions that they be sent to friends and family of the prisoners. The Germans were adamant that the cards, pre-printed with suitable phrases like 'arrived safe and sound' and 'best regards' and in no way headed either 'Auschwitz' or 'Birkenau', but 'Am Waldsee', which was a resort town located near the Swiss border. The cards were duly sent and many thousands of replies ensued. The replies were not delivered because the addressees were burnt before the replies could be. This was another German ruse, the purpose of which was to allay the fears of the public at large and put an end to the rumours that were rife about camps like Auschwitz.

Another instance of the pure theatre involved in the Nazi running of Auschwitz, told to Mayer by his best friend, David Josefowicz, was the delivery from outside of the mauve coloured pea sized pellets of the granulated substance, Zyclon B. The Prussic acid contained in this solid chemical turned into highly lethal hydrogen cyanide gas when it came into contact with air, unleashing a bitter, almond-like odour. The scandalous element of this daily procedure was that the gas forming material was brought in a car bearing the insignia of the International Red Cross. Zyclon B was never held in stock in the crematorium and for every batch of Jews gassed, the Red Cross car would arrive bringing an SS officer and a Deputy Health Officer, the latter holding four green canisters. Walking across the grass he would pour a canister into each of four short concrete pipes rising from the ground, each about thirty yards distant from the last one. Within five minutes everybody in the chambers was dead. In order to ensure the successful conclusion to their work, the two gas butchers would wait another five minutes. They would then light up their cigarettes and drive off. The net result of their action was to have just killed three thousand innocent victims in half the time required by carbon monoxide, a fact that the commandant of Auschwitz, Rudolf Hoess, admitted being greatly excited by. Since the Germans had considered the Jews to be no better than vermin, it was an ironic fact indeed when an insecticide proved to be the most efficient eliminator of their race.

"You seemed to be so organised, Mayer, in your own strategy for survival, can you give a list of your survival strategies and explain how and why each played a part in you living beyond the cessation of hostilities?"

"I was not prepared to take unnecessary risks in any escape attempts as, in most cases, it was futile because the odds against you were infinite and you would most certainly have been caught, beaten and hanged as a public spectacle. I subconsciously devised different strategies for I recognised my limitations. I was never as robust physically as my brother, Yakov and I reasoned within these confines. The foreman or civilian engineer would watch you most diligently and, if you were caught resting for even a second or two, a severe beating would ensue. These beatings all went toward sapping what little strength you may have had at the time. Once caught by the supervisor in this way, you would then automatically attract unwelcome attention and be carefully monitored. I wanted to live and to stand any chance of achieving this seemingly impossible dream, I knew I had to be most observant. I knew I had to be aware from the corners of my eyes of the whereabouts of both foreman and civilian engineer, for in some cases the latter could be the more sadistic of the two. A prime example of my lack of observation letting me down was when I had befriended the Hitler youth, who had begun to be a vital source of raw potatoes. Failure on my part to identify the position of the engineer one particular day extinguished immediately my newfound source of extra food and extra hope. The rules for survival changed depending on the type of work on which you were engaged, piece work being a prime example. When filling or emptying rail wagons or lorries, whoever finished last would receive a brutal punishment, so in this instance it paid to work that little bit harder, it paid to be competitive. When filling trolleys with soil, we had to push them on a narrow gauge rail to a position where, with careful balance and no little skill, we would tip the material without allowing the trolley to fall down the ravine. Should this happen, and it did on several occasions, this would be construed as sabotage and a cruel beating and/or death would follow."

In August 1943 a joyous surprise lay in wait for Mayer when a friend, Arek Hersh, observed Yakov, Mayer's elder brother arriving at the quarantine camp in Birkenau. His chest burst with joy at the sight of Yakov still alive. The two brothers talked excitedly at the wire with Mayer receiving a savage beating from an SS guard brandishing a thin whip, but he thought it well worth while being able to converse with possibly the only other close family member still alive. Eventually Yakov moved to the same camp that housed Mayer, where he was put in the Potato Kommandos, in charge of which were the black uniformed Ukraine guards, so incredibly brutal and significantly worse than the German SS. There were ten thousand SS troops working shifts covering Auschwitz-Birkenau and they had their own kitchen and food specially prepared for them. Acute hunger drove Yakov to steal a potato on more than one occasion but he was usually caught and beaten badly, for potatoes were not for prisoners and only for the ten thousand strong SS army at Auschwitz. Yakov's philosophy on survival deemed the risk of a beating worth it when hunger was extreme. The work was incredibly hard, running with heavy barrels of potatoes, and, being under the control of the most brutal guards in the entire Birkenau complex, the intensely anti-Semitic Ukrainians, the life of most Jews in this Kommando would be very limited. These Ukrainian guards generally could speak little if any German and, whilst their native tongue and Polish were reasonably akin, French and German Jews would not understand many of the commands and their miserable existence would be compounded by even more beatings. Considering all this extreme cruelty Mayer advised Yakov to change his commando and work with his younger brother. Mayer knew the foreman, name of Katz, who came from Zdunska Wola and asked him not to beat his elder brother.

With curfew in the camp set at nine pm, the best chance the two brothers had of talking to each other was after work. On only one occasion, and that only for two days, did the two work together, when they were involved in the unloading and assembling of barracks in the 'Mexico' camp, so large by that time, that it was virtually the same size as camp D. By this time Mayer had caught up with his brother's passage thus far in the mayhem that was Jewish captivity in Nazi dominated Europe. Back in December 1939, Yakov had found himself in the company of a large group of friends and acquaintances from Sieradz as they made their way to their first camp, Rawicz, on the pre-war German-Polish border. The work to which they were put, both there and in a few more related sub camps in the same region, consisted mainly of cleaning up rivers and building embankments. The tasks were arduous and exacting on starvation rations. Willy, the foreman guard at Rawicz, brought back excruciating memories to Yakov for his particular brand of wanton brutality. In some of these sub camps the Hitler jugend (Hitler youth) were in charge and rejoiced in expressing their hatred of the Jews by beating the prisoners with sadistic delight. On one such occasion when Yakov was caught resting on his shovel for a few seconds, the Hitler youth hit him so hard that frustration and anger made him respond by landing his shovel on the youth's head. Consequently all hell was let loose and Yakov was beaten to a pulp, passing out and nearly dying. Subsequently taken by horse and cart to the police station, he was questioned at length as to why he hit the Hitler youth and told in no uncertain terms that the committing of such a crime attracted the sentence of death by hanging. Mayer's elder brother feared his life was at an end but, when offering to clean and repair the policemen's bicycles, this service became so convenient to his minders that not only was his life spared, but also he was allowed to eat any scraps of food left over by his custodians. He found himself starting to put on a little weight, totally unheard of in those times for anybody of his faith, but unfortunately the respite was only temporary and he was returned to the camp.

Mayer knew Yakov was much stronger physically than himself but doubted if he could take excessive beatings, so, with this in mind, he suggested that Yakov's best chance of survival lay in working down a coalmine rather than with the Potato Kommandos. Although some prisoners died from accidents, the advice was well founded for food in the coal mine was slightly better than in Auschwitz. Good fortune smiled on Yakov when his offer to volunteer for duty in coalmining was accepted and he was shipped from Auschwitz to the Jawozno mine, just north from that notorious camp from hell. Work in the mine was incredibly hard with long shifts amidst dangerously unsafe conditions. The carrot that was to continue to maintain his striving for survival was undoubtedly the marginally superior food ration, although many inmates died or were so physically worn out that they were returned to Auschwitz for gassing. Around the 15th of January 1945 with the Soviet forces getting ever closer, approximately five thousand Jews from all the Silesian coalmines, the richest source in the whole of Poland for this particular raw material, were taken on a death march through deep snow without food or water in temperatures around minus twenty two degrees. Many prisoners died, most of whom were shot by the SS guards, before the much diminished line of stragglers arrived at a camp called Blachammer situated near Gleiwitz. There the ever enterprising Yakov removed some bricks from the barrack wall and, together with some friends, escaped. Some were shot, so near, and yet so far from freedom, and only Mayer's brother and a couple of others managed to hide up in a hay barn until the Russians liberated them on the 27th of the same month. When the two brothers met up years after the war Yakov admitted that Mayer's advice saved his life.

Mayer knew he would have died in a coalmine, he knew his limitations and he went for comparatively easier work and where he knew the foreman. He was aware that, in order to survive, he had to give the impression of being a good worker, avoid beatings and keep a sharp eye out for the foreman at all times. He would survive each day by watching most diligently.

On one occasion inside Birkenau, Mayer was alone, on his knees scrubbing a very long cement barrack floor when suddenly a drunken SS man, a friend of the absent block leader, stumbled in and took a fancy to him with respect to further tormenting the wretched creature. The German said, "Jew, get out!" drawing his gun from the holster, Mayer thought his time was up and there was nothing he could do about it, for he dare not plead with the Nazi. He made him run around outside the barracks, Mayer's mind anticipating the end and questioning how he could reason with a drunken SS man when he couldn't reason with a sober one? Again suddenly the German snapped, "stop", and replaced his gun in the holster. He proceeded to give Mayer several lashes with his thick leather belt across the backside. Beating a person with some flesh still on his carcass was painful to the recipient, but when men were merely skin and bone the pain was much greater, bone protesting very much so against pain, which lasted longer. Mayer knew he was still alive for he could feel the pain. It constituted pure entertainment for the master race, exhibiting total domination over Jews.

All the time at Auschwitz, eighteen months in all, the stench of burning flesh permeated all over the site, being fuelled by fire and smoke belching out day and night from the four tall crematoria chimneys. The Jews could tell in part who was in the majority being burnt, for people fresh from home who still had generously covered frames produced a smell characteristic of burning flesh, whilst bodies worked to death in the camps were totally emaciated skin and bone and they smelt just like rags.

"You have mentioned more than once that being able to understand the German language was vital. Why did speaking German save your life?"

"I was able to understand the guard's orders instantly and this knowledge saved me from many more beatings and minimising their number directly influenced the chances of survival. I witnessed many prisoners of varying nationalities having the life beaten out of their hapless bodies due to their inability to pick up quickly enough on the Nazi ravings."

Mayer and his colleagues from D camp could see the new arrivals at the rail head and it became clear from watching them closely that they didn't have a clue at which place they had arrived nor did they know what was going to happen to them. They could see mothers holding children by the hand and sometimes babies in their arms marching off to the gas chambers, where in an hour or two they would all be dead. In fact, about ninety percent of new Jews were dead within an hour of arrival, most of whom, because the chambers resembled shower rooms, would only realise the hand they had been dealt when the hydrogen cyanide started polluting their enclosed space, making the Nazis' job that much easier. Auschwitz was anything but welcoming, psychologically barren, offering prisoners no hope, nothing that would give inmates the remotest inkling of a future.

Barren also with respect to vegetation, for the starving Jews had eaten most of the grass whenever they were able. The soil at Birkenau was of clay in nature and, in days of heavy rainfall, the relatively flat land was prone to flood, the very threat of which gave rise to yet another job for the Jews and one on which Mayer worked, the building of improvised drainage systems running alongside the road which proved most successful. In what could be high Polish summer temperatures, the clay dried to a very hard abrasive base which caused prisoners wearing wooden clogs great discomfort and pain. There was no give in these clogs, worn incidentally not only by Dutch Jews but also numerous other races, and the feet, always without socks, would rub badly enough to prevent a person from marching. This meant inability to go to work, which meant automatic selection for death. Mayer was given shoes, for which he was eternally grateful, but possibly others preferred wooden clogs for extra warmth. The sight of hapless Jews shuffling along in clogs was a great source of amusement to the Germans, who knew that sore feet thus produced meant an inevitable ticket to the gas chambers.

"If there was one thing you could change in all this experience, what would it be?"

"Ideally, that the Holocaust had never happened."

"Considering your religious upbringing, how did you manage to keep your faith whilst witnessing, all around you, indescribable atrocities?"

"With the greatest of difficulty is the short answer. Seeing babies and very young children, all totally innocent of any crime, being forced to walk with their mothers to the gas chambers, made me ask why would God allow this to happen? I decided not to ask any more questions because

105

humans had performed these dreadful deeds, not God. But why hadn't the outside world done something about this den of iniquity. They knew, for there had been two successful escapes, there were train drivers, lorry drivers. The world knows now from the wartime records, when Britain was able to break the German Enigma code, all the gruesome details on an almost daily basis were revealed. They all knew but why was there no compassionate action taken then, to perhaps relieve our suffering somewhat and perhaps give a chance for more of us to survive. I cannot forgive this lack of action from the free world. Maybe politics and expediency had something to do with it. Let us hope that the leaders in the free world will have learnt a vital lesson. If any prejudice or hatred should manifest itself anywhere towards the Jewish people, why shouldn't understanding and fairness be the gentile world's response."

Next to Mayer's camp was a gypsy camp, they were unusually allowed to live there as whole families. This seems doubly strange when one considers that the Third Reich had declared them an inferior race and, as such, had been herded together from all the occupied countries into Auschwitz, the ultimate extermination centre. They were allowed to remain together as families because, some suggested, they were Catholics and, although they did not work, were given the responsibility of policing the neighbouring Jewish camps and barracks, where they exercised their new found authority with unimaginable cruelty. Two other reasons why gypsies were kept together, since they had already been classified as sub human, the convenience it afforded when the day of extermination dawned, as well as the availability of suitable subjects for Dr Mengele's experimentation programme. Other Christians with families were separated because they were not for destruction, as were the Jews. This category of prisoner could be trade unionists, Communists and mostly German political prisoners perceived to be anti Nazis. The Germans tended to view this group with some suspicion, looking on them in the context that if they were not for them, they most certainly must be against them. These Christians' wives and children would be left at home and their menfolk put through 'Umlehrung', which means re-education. In effect there was no education taking place, merely persecution and brutalities, most of these political prisoners being incarcerated before the war in camps such as Dacchau and Buchenwald. There were two so called political prisoners in 24D, the first a true blooded German criminal, a genial man of good company who had the audacity to escape in order to go for a drink before being recaptured and returned to the same barrack. Providing such a person kept a reasonably low profile, his birthright would virtually guarantee his surviving the war. The second person was the German Jew block leader who exhibited a red triangle signifying a political prisoner and probably the yellow star of the Jews, although Mayer cannot remember seeing this mark of the accursed faith. No matter, for the odds against this Jew surviving were many times more than those for the common German criminal.

In April 1944 there was a double curfew in D camp and they knew something sinister was going to happen soon. Confirming their fears, in April 1944 a man in the Sonderkommandos, literal meaning kommandos assigned to special work, told the tall Polish Jew block leader from Mayer's barrack of the German plan to eliminate each and every one of the gypsies. Mayer knew of this oppressive measure before anyone else because, as he was scrubbing the barrack floor nearby, his sharp hearing and excellent understanding of German enabled him to understand the SS man's message to the block leader. Scores of lorries arrived and all the gypsies were loaded onto them. These unfortunates anticipated something bad was about to envelop them and they were most reluctant to get into the lorries. They were beaten brutally and their cries could be heard a distance away but all to no avail, in fact next morning all the gypsies were dead. Approximately four thousand five hundred were taken which emptied that camp in readiness for many huge shipments of Jews from Hungary and the ghetto of Lodz. The extermination process was apparently similar to that used previously during the liquidation of a Czech camp. All the barracks were quarantined and SS guards with dogs emptied the gypsy quarters and lined them up before handing to them rations of bread and salami. This was a clever German trick to try to allay any fears within the gypsy ranks and to add credence to the Aryan statement that they were being moved to another camp. After all, why distribute food when recipients were bound for the gas chambers? It was a deception conceived in order to calm the masses and produce a rapid and smooth exit of a large number of people under the auspices of a relatively small guard. Mayer will always remember the gut wrenching screams of these doomed Christians, some of the gypsies at least were not convinced by the Germans' sham of a humanitarian act.

"You cheated Dr Mengele in his life or death selections on at least forty occasions. What did you think it felt like to be selected for the gas chambers?"

"A boy of similar age to me and who worked alongside

me was incredibly angry that he had been chosen. He turned around abruptly on me, challenging me with the question, "why me and not you? I look no worse than you". Others were almost relieved to be selected, for they had reached the point that they could take no more and perhaps didn't fancy the alternative of walking into the electrified fence. Some would be struck with fear at the thought of the choking sensation and the futile fight to the top of the pile, searching for cleaner air and that extra minute or two of life. An individual's reaction at such a traumatic moment as this had to be a very personal one. I am a great believer in the fact that a person had to experience a happening to have valuable comment on that happening. Primo Levi, in his book *'If This Is A Man'* put it admirably. *'We, the survivors, are not the true witnesses. The true witnesses, those that is, in full possession of the terrible truth, are the drowned, the submerged, the annihilated. They were not merely destroyed, they were blotted out of existence, we speak in their stead by proxy'."*

When the hundreds of thousands of Hungarian Jews started arriving at Auschwitz on the 16th May 1944, they all came clutching chicken and sausages, good food and plenty of it, no doubt with the encouragement of the Germans, who probably sold them the story of resettling them in a better homeland. This was undoubtedly true, for the Nazis also asked them to bring timber under the pretext of settling in the east. In effect the timber was to be used for cremating the bodies that had been previously gassed. The Horthy Government in Hungary was extremely anti-Semitic and, with the Hungarian police totally committed to the efficient rounding up of the Jews, two to five trains would arrive daily from all parts of Hungary, each train consisting of forty to fifty goods vans, with one hundred people crammed into each and every van. This extermination of huge numbers of Hungarian Jews continued without interruption until the middle of September 1944. On some days a greater number of transports would arrive and then the closed vans packed with prisoners had to stop at the railway sidings for several hours, sometimes in unbearably hot summer temperatures of thirty degrees and freezing winter temperatures of twenty two degrees below. All this in cattle trucks awash in urine and excrement, accompanied by the stench of human bodies and quicklime strewn on the floor as a disinfectant with the urine dripping out of closed doors amid the petrified screams from those inside. The trains were often subjected to long delays thereby extending the misery and accentuating the humiliation. Thirst was possibly the worst punishment of all, bringing piercing screams from inmates packed like the proverbial sardines, some prisoners telling of desperate mothers giving their children urine to quiet their thirst. Russian POWs helped with the unloading of the never-ending line of food parcels from a land where there was no shortage of food and quality food at that. Mayer watched the operation from behind his own wire when, suddenly, one of the Russians, who was known to him, hissed in his native tongue surreptitiously, "catch these and we'll share". Mayer's natural guarded caution on the wider subject of survival cried out in the negative. His mind was in turmoil, on the face of it the prospect was sheer madness but, he was conscious of becoming increasingly weaker due to diminishing food rations with its attendant threat of failing a selection. He nervously glanced around, there were no guards in the immediate vicinity and he instantly recognised that this was an occasion worth taking a chance. The Russian threw the food over the fence, Mayer catching it and depositing the trophies in a safe hiding place on his person before sharing with the Russian at the end of the day. This high-risk venture lasted about three days and that gamble probably helped him survive the last few months of Auschwitz, although it did nothing for his already frayed nerves. As a matter of interest he only learned two words in Hungarian during the remainder of his stay, they were 'food' and 'yes'.

"To most people the Germans come across as highly organised people when dealing with economic measures. How did this show itself in relation to their treatment of the Jews?"

"In destroying European Jews the Nazis realised they had an incredible bounty within their grasp and, believe you me, they wasted nothing. Initially they took over thriving Jewish businesses, invaded and pillaged countless homes and finally wrung every last advantage out of men and women capable of work. In Auschwitz there was a collection of barracks known as 'Canada' where literally anything of the remotest economical use or value was stored. In different huts there would be spectacles, human hair, shoes and boots, portmanteaus and luggage cases of every size, clothing, nothing, but nothing, was wasted. The first dividend the prisoners received from the Third Reich was the lice in the camp clothing, very probably from the previous two or three owners. The food the Jews received was just sufficient to keep them from dying for days or weeks, but insufficient to keep them really alive. They had no albumin in their systems, causing their legs to become as heavy as lead and, with no fats, their bodies swelled. Migraines and nosebleeds were common, whilst lack of vitamin B caused regular drowsiness and some amnesia. The Germans considered every possible aspect in improving economic efficiency, even down to measuring the combustibility of various types of coke and corpses. They eventually concluded that the best oven mix consisted of one well nourished, fast burning adult, one child and one emaciated adult already reduced to skin and bone by starvation and hard labour. Not content with this means of saving, SS Sergeant-Major Otto Moll, overseer of all the crematoria, relentlessly pursued his own fanatically gruesome economics. In new crematorium pits he had Jews digging out drainage channels that were sloped so that the fat from burning bodies would run down and collect in pans. That fat could then be poured back on to the fire to make it burn faster, thereby saving the Nazis valuable coke supplies. Thus even the Jews' own fat was used to save the Third Reich money. The economics didn't even end there, for after cremation, Jewish bones were ground into meal and spread as fertiliser over the German earth to enrich the German crops that went to fill the German bellies."

It is well chronicled that Auschwitz totally broke the Jewish spirit and pictures of the mentally broken hordes meekly trudging toward the gas chambers has often brought well meaning suggestions of why didn't they try to take a German with them. They were going to die anyway, so why not? Such a theoretical observation is easily reached when not in the confines of that demoralising camp, apart from which, perhaps death was such a merciful relief that the masses were only too resigned to meet their maker. Whatever one's view of that calamitous situation, when there was any resistance to the Nazis within Auschwitz, news spread faster than a forest fire on the wind. On two occasions there was such resistance and, although not witnessed by Mayer himself, these slaps in the face for the Germans, together with the knowledge by then that the enemy was fighting a losing cause, helped boost Jewish morale no end. The first instance occurred after the arrival of a shipment of prisoners from the Warsaw ghetto and a group of naked females were being collected together en route to the gas chambers. One particularly strikingly beautiful young Jewish actress caught the eye of one of the SS guards and he raped her. In the struggle that accompanied the act, the lady managed to get his pistol out of its holster and she shot him dead. It didn't do her any good, for she was gassed within minutes but, spiritually, she had made a statement.

The second act of resistance was on a much larger scale and involved the Sonderkommandos, sometimes referred to as the 'kommandos of the living dead', for these strong and fit Jews worked within the gas chambers and the crematoria. Their job was physically demanding and consequently their food ration was significantly more than the pittance given to Jews employed in all other areas of the complex. The Sonderkommandos saw everything that the Germans wanted to hide from the outside world and consequently every four months their entire squad, numbering some eight hundred and fifty three would be exterminated. The twelfth group knew their time was coming to an end and they had secretly planned to go down fighting. The operation had been carefully planned for some time with the women from the Unio explosives factory smuggling in their products. Mayer was to find out much later a lot of the details of the operation from his closest friend, David Josefowicz, who was aware of the plot well in advance due to his roving maintenance duties on the plant.

In the immediately preceding days before that day of attempted retribution, 7th October 1944, a hundred boxes of high explosives had reached the Sonder camp from that same Unio munitions plant that employed Polish Jews as workers. David himself had smuggled explosives in to the Sonderkommandos over a period of time, underneath the false bottoms of soup barrels.

October 6th 1944 was the last but one day of the 12th Sonderkommandos allotted life span and the escape plan had been fine tuned to enable the escaping Jews to head for the loop in the Vistula river, the home of countless volumes of ash from the cremating of Jews, and only two kilometres distant. The river would be at a low level in October and could be forded with comparative ease and from this point a mere eight kilometres separated them from vast forests stretching all the way to the far flung regions of Poland. These dense undergrowths would enable the escaping prisoners to see the war out and hopefully meet up with the Partisans to help rid Europe of the Nazi menace. Number one crematorium was the only one of the four working on the sixth of October and that would cease work at eighteen hundred hours, which meant the Sonderkommando night shift would not be needed and the SS guards would not be as diligent as normal. Consequently it made good sense to arrange the escape for the night of the sixth.

One can only imagine the shock and horror on the faces of the would be escapees when, at approximately fourteen thirty hours, there was a thunderous explosion from number three crematorium and sirens wailed their haunting echoes over Auschwitz-Birkenau. Something had gone terribly wrong for the timing was about ten to eleven hours early.

What could it be? Was there a traitor in the camp? The apprehension in the air after all that careful planning must have been so incredibly intense. As with many well laid plans, something totally unexpected occurred and was not caused by treason of any kind. At around fourteen hundred hours a truck-load of political SS arrived at crematorium number three and, when their commandant ordered the Sonderkommandos to assemble, nobody moved. He then went on to turn on the Nazi charm by telling his charges that they were sending them to a rest camp with good clothes, plenty to eat and life a little easier. This sounded too good to be true, another of the hollow Nazi promises designed merely to appease the inmates and guarantee the minimum of disturbance to the Third Reich in moving another batch of expendable Jews from A to B. This was the end, this was indeed their end and the 12th Sonderkommandos knew it. The ruse had appeared to work for, on his reading out of the Hungarian prisoner numbers, those newest of the Birkenau international collection, responded promptly by lining up and were duly taken to camp D barrack 13. These were followed on to the square by the Greeks and then it was the Poles to be assembled. When the commandant called out a certain Polish number, a bottle seemingly of mineral water, thrown by another Pole, landed at the commandant's feet, the explosion killing him and injuring or killing six others. The mutiny had started early but there was no going back. The Greeks were mown down in the courtyard and then came that enormous explosion in that same crematorium number three, burying alive the Sonderkommandos inside who were firing on the SS.

On hearing the explosion from crematorium three, the men working the ovens in crematorium one left their posts, with the SS guard questioning their action. In order to rapidly restore order, he hit two men with the curved end of his cane, the second drawing his knife and stabbing the SS guard to death. As he fell two Sonderkommandos threw him head first into the ovens. Drawn by the crowd, a second SS guard met a similar fate and joined his colleague, their four boots being all there was of them sticking from the oven. Open warfare then commenced in number one, with machine guns, hand grenades and boxes of dynamite being quickly broken out of a secret store; one hand grenade had the distinction of killing seven SS and wounding others. The Sonderkommandos fought a tough rearguard action before pouring out through the back gates of crematorium number one, firing as they went. A hole had already been cut in the electrified barbed wire fence with a specially insulated pair of cutters and, although the Germans knew immediately of the breakthrough and acted accordingly, the prisoners swept through the gap, making for the loop in the Vistula. Soon afterwards, the Germans gained the upper hand through superior manpower and immense material advantages. All the dead from crematoria two, three and four, together with prisoners who had fallen outside the wire, were all brought back to crematorium one to be processed. David Josefowicz, sensing all was lost and with the Germans shooting to kill any Jews in the immediate area, dodged back to his camp unseen and, as such, saved his own life. Lady luck had smiled once again on his best friend and great risk taker, the differences in character between the two school chums being extremely diverse.

Twelve Sonderkommandos crossed the Vistula and rested

at the house of one who, it transpired, was a collaborator.

Their betrayal being a particularly bitter pill to take after all the efforts of so many to get eye witnesses out to the free world to reveal the truth of the Nazi atrocities. The twelve survivors were brought back to number one crematorium but, on arrival and on a certain signal arranged between themselves, laid into the guards for their weapons. They fought viciously and bravely with all they had, their bare fists, and gave the SS a severe mauling. To no avail however, for weapons obviously won the day and all twelve were shot. Of the fact they died a hero's death there could be no doubt. Unfortunately after so much effort and loss of life, nobody had succeeded in escaping to tell the world the full despicable story of Auschwitz-Birkenau. It had been a magnificent failure from which accrued the following positive achievements: 70 SS personnel dead, number three crematorium burnt to the ground and the severely damaged equipment in number four crematorium effectively rendered it useless. The price paid was the lives of the 853 Sonderkommandos, who bravely gave everything in a bid for freedom and a strike against tyranny. The seven surviving members of the twelfth Sonderkommandos were the doctors and medical assistants who assisted Dr Mengele and who were not involved in the uprising.

Auschwitz was the most indescribable hell ever constructed by man, with SS officers enjoying taunting prisoners, with the spirit and the guts to dream of escaping, by saying, "the only exit is up the chimney". Some inmates described the camp as being of 'another planet', an SS doctor named Heinz Thilo preferred the descriptive phrase, 'anus mundi', the anus of the world, whilst others referred to Birkenau as the graveyard of millions but with not one gravestone. Another SS doctor who also took part in selections, Dr Johann Kremer, described Auschwitz after being present at his first 'action' against the Jews. "By comparison Dante's inferno seems almost a comedy, Auschwitz is justly called an extermination camp!"

Mayer's father arrived in Birkenau at the end of August 1944 after two years slave labour in the ghetto of Lodz and he was taken straight to the gas chambers. Mayer's sister, Kajla, also arrived with him and she was taken away and allowed to stay at Auschwitz for a few days before being sent to Stutthof.

Mayer was also to be sent to Stutthof while his sister was still there but they never met for men and women were never allowed to mix. Kajla was most unfortunate when, in January 1945 in a bitterly cold Polish winter, the Germans put her together with one thousand other women on a ship which they subsequently scuttled in ice cold Baltic waters. Not one of them survived and his sister died at the tender age of twenty four years. He discovered these scraps of information regarding his father and sister many years after cessation of hostilities, in fact only after the bringing down of the Berlin Wall.

Christmas 1944 was a time in Auschwitz when rumours and counter rumours circulated as quickly as the bitterly cold winds dragged the temperatures down to new lows. With the Germans very much on the back foot at this time and with a doubtful future ahead, the grapevine reported that their hosts had installed a Christmas tree in the women's camp. "Were the Nazis attempting to make peace with the prisoners they had used and abused?" the inmates pondered. Their conjectures were shattered by disillusionment when the Germans produced four women who, they claimed, had been involved in smuggling explosives for the Sonderkommando escape attempt two and a half months earlier. On January 4th 1945, within yards of the Christmas tree, they hanged the four hapless females, two at a time in order that both shifts could witness the reprisals to those who allegedly had assisted the prisoners to make the bravest of statements on that October day in 1944. Far from showing goodwill at this appropriate period, the Germans persisted with their torment of the Jews, as always, dressed in a public spectacle.

In order to realise how major a part Auschwitz played in Jewish extermination and also how proud the Nazi hierarchy were of their level of achievement, one has only to consider the experience of the late Vera Atkins. This lady, born Vera Maria Rosenberg in Romania on June 15th 1907, rose to become the brilliant assistant to Colonel Maurice Buckmaster at the French section of the Special Operations Executive, working up to 18 hours a day at the section's headquarters at 64 Baker Street, London. The confessions she obtained from Rudolf Hoess, the former Commandant of Auschwitz, were later used as evidence during the Nuremberg Trials, one factual statement of his putting the maximum capacity of Auschwitz-Birkenau at one hundred and forty thousand prisoners. She could later hardly bring herself to recall how Hoess had reacted to the suggestion that the deaths in his camp had perhaps amounted to 1,500,000. "Oh no," he retorted, as if he had been sadly misrepresented, "it was 2,345,000."

To further emphasise the special classification that Auschwitz, above any of the other camps, descended into, let us consider the words of Lord Russell of Liverpool, a Judge in the Nazi wartime crimes trial at Nuremberg. In his book *'The Scourge Of The Swastika'*, he wrote of Auschwitz in the following vein: *'were everything to be written, it would not be read, if read it would not be believed'*.

Chapter Eight

As the Russians were approaching Auschwitz, Mayer and other Jews were moved north to the port of Stutthof, near Gdansk in East Prussia, in accordance with the Nazi decree that no Jewish slave labourers should be allowed to be liberated by Allied forces. This measure was to ensure that no testimonies of the brutal treatment meted out to Jews would permeate through to the free world. The concentration camp at Stutthof was opened by the Nazis on September 2nd 1939, only one day after entering the Free City of Danzig and annexing it to the German Reich. It was in the area around Stutthof that the Germans, in the Spring of 1944, had begun to set up sixty new labour camps to replace those further east that had been overrun by Soviet forces. Conditions were barbaric, tens of thousands of prisoners dying of dysentery, typhus and starvation. Many others were brutally clubbed to death while working in nearby forests, or sadistically drowned in mud; some met their maker via phenol injections and their bodies burned in the crematorium, in specially designed high capacity ovens.

There was no food or water provided on the three day journey to Stutthof and the pathetic cargo, for that was how the Nazis viewed the Jews, had no idea to where they were being sent. Their destination was indicated on the outside of the cattle truck but the slave labourers were only to ascertain that fact when they arrived. The German SS were in charge of Stutthof, which was both a concentration and extermination camp, hosting mostly Jews but also some non-Jews. To say the sizeable barracks at Stutthof were primitive would be an understatement, the bunk beds had no mattresses and the food was meagre comprising one tiny piece of bread per day. At the beginning of November 1944 it was incredibly cold and unloading bricks by throwing one at a time to your partner soon resulted in an absence of skin on men's hands, for no gloves were supplied. The camp was surrounded by a barbed wire fence and, to Mayer's knowledge, nobody escaped. The work also involved unloading and moving heavy cement bags and, should one of these emaciated shadows drop a bag through a combination of malnutrition and exhaustion, they would receive a severe beating. The only other job he was used on at Stutthof involved the unloading of horse manure, an easily worked medium which represented, probably the least physically taxing, of all the hard labours.

There was repair and maintenance work at Stutthof and most of the guards wore the black uniform of the Ukrainian, Latvian or Lithuanian SS. The Germans liked the collaborators from these three countries because of their brutal nature and yet didn't trust them totally. In Lithuania, the black shirted SS killed many Jews, having a real passion for it, and would just leave the corpses where they dropped. This sloppy practice annoyed the totally organised German SS and they told the Lithuanians to dispose of the bodies, thereby hiding the evidence. The Eastern European's retort was, "who do you think we are? Labourers? The Germans sent the Wehrmacht in but some agreed to the clearing up operation and some didn't. The SS reported the Wehrmacht refusal to Berlin and High Command ordered the Wehrmacht to clear the bodies, which was duly done.

When there was no job available to be done, Jews would be chased around the camp square by SS guards wielding horsewhips. There would be about one hundred Jews being driven around the large open area and, if one was not quick enough or failed to maintain a position on the outer edge, one would feel the pain from the business end of the lash. Never should time be wasted when it could be used to torment Jews. This chastised race was to be tormented twenty-four hours a day, even through the entire night. There were no medals for ill treating Jews, only deep satisfaction and fulfilment for the Nazi regime.

One day the slave labourers couldn't believe their eyes as disarmed German soldiers, devoid of their belts and caps, were shepherded on the other side of the wire into the adjacent camp, and indeed, later into Mayer's camp. "Why are you here? What crime have you committed?," the perplexed Jews couldn't wait to ask the questions. Apparently these Nazi soldiers had asked their army authorities where were they going. Because they had asked this question, they were treated as suspect prisoners and were obviously bound for the Eastern front, which, at that time, was an experience infinitely worse than death. The approximately fifty to one hundred Germans were still at Stutthof when the Jews were moved to yet another camp. It was a joy to the Jews to see the anxiety in the eyes of the Germans, and Mayer, with his good standard of German, was one of those prisoners asking questions of their tormentors. Opinions differed with respect to the treatment they might expect from the imminent liberation by the Russians. Some argued the Russians might be lenient because they'd rebelled in some way against the Nazi cause. Others knew at first hand about the barbaric and totally

123

unforgiving feeling between the Russians and the Germans. Far from being sent to the Eastern front, that challenging front was coming to them real fast, accompanied by an intensely cold wind blowing from the Baltic Sea.

Unbeknown to Mayer, another member of the Herszkowicz family had already become familiar with the obnoxious qualities of Stutthof, for his sister, Kajla, had arrived at Stutthof as early as the 4th of September 1944. However, due to the strict enforcement of the no mixing of the sexes rule, brother and sister were never to meet, Mayer moving on to his sixth camp in mid December 1944.

Chapter Nine

After a short time, again with the Russians getting ever closer, they were forced into cattle trucks without any heating in mid December 1944; it was bitterly cold on that journey with many suffering agonies through frostbite and chilblains. Suddenly the weather changed and it became milder and the terrible itching started. One prisoner in the truck advised the others not to take their shoes off because, if they started scratching, open wounds would result, feet would start swelling up and it would not be possible to put the shoes back on again. Those who listened lived a little longer, those who didn't, perished. The five-day trip, like all the previous journeys, was neither accompanied by food nor water. Due to people's insides by now being totally empty the bucket supplied by the Germans for the sanitary needs of each packed cattle truck was used less and less. They eventually arrived at Echterdingen military airfield, twelve kilometres from Stuttgart in south west Germany, Mayer's sixth camp, and were housed in an aircraft hangar. It was extremely cold due to the massive doors never being able to be shut properly and many of the prisoners had snow on their bunk beds. Prior to their arrival the camp was empty but when the contingency arrived there were 750 men and, after a matter of about eight weeks, only 280 were still left alive. Some of his colleagues died from starvation, beatings, extreme hard work and some were deliberately clubbed to death because they had the misfortune to have gold teeth. Jewish inmates were forced to dig graves to house their unfortunate brothers in a compound within the camp during the night, this by no means mirroring the normal German practice of counting the bodies before shipping them out to be cremated. Fraudulent practices were rife at this stage of the war as the German guards didn't report these Jews who were clubbed to death, in order to maintain the higher level of food allocation, selling the surplus on the black market. SS guards didn't feel as accountable as previously with the war approaching its final months.

At Stuttgart, for most of the time, they were put to work at a nearby stone quarry, run by civilian engineers, but, so low were the temperatures, the gelignite would merely jump out of the ground and not break up the terrain as required. The freezing temperatures killed many of the scantily clad, impoverished prisoners, for the miserly food rations were no more than at Auschwitz, although the level of torment was by no means as high as in the Silesian death camp. The surviving Jews were later used on the repair of bomb damaged roads, Stuttgart by now receiving an incredible pounding every night, the constant air raids acting as a great morale booster for the skeletal Jewish labourers.

Chapter Ten

As the Allies were approaching Stuttgart in mid February 1945 the approximately two hundred and eighty remaining Jews were taken out and sent off to Gotha, camp number seven, in the traditional transport reserved for Jews, cattle trucks, the journey taking about twenty-four hours. On arrival the bunkers were full of ammunition and consequently their first night saw them put up in very old houses in the town, which were derelict and devoid of floor coverings and even menial furniture, later discovered to be part of the Jewish ghetto, which had long since been liquidated. The degree of dereliction of the property could best be judged by the fact that non-Jews had not taken over the buildings as they had done in numerous other communities. The occasion was the first time he had not spent a night in a camp barrack or cattle truck for no less than four years eleven months. The fact that innocent Jews had once lived there made for a flood of memories of his own close family and their probable demise. Consequently an uneasy broken sleep ensued. The following day, after removing all the ammunition, they experienced the damp and the cold of their new home, bunk beds underground in the bunkers within the Weimar forest, well concealed from Allied bombers. Because this was directly part of the last throes of the German war effort, they were expected to load and unload ammunition extremely quickly and yet carefully, considering the nature of their product. They were very badly treated with the military SS in charge, performing physically demanding tasks literally around the clock, achieved with living carcasses long rendered incapable of such effort. And yet, inconceivably, most managed the impossible, obviously spurred on by the living dream that the end might just be in sight. Since their work was most important to the German war effort, one might have thought that the food level may have been increased slightly but, on the contrary, miniscule quantities were less than in previous camps. The thought had crossed Mayer's mind that possibly the Germans were beginning to run short of provisions but he discounted that theory when he remembered the German mentality toward the Jews. His race were only there in order that the Aryan masters extract the maximum useful work out of their pathetic carcasses, prior to their total elimination from this earth. The latter reason was why they left Auschwitz, Stutthof and Stuttgart when they did, always just ahead of the arrival of the dreaded Russians. They could have eliminated the Jews at any of these camps but they wanted to see the last vestige of energy wrung from their skin and bone and the attendant pleasure that brought. This greed to maximise the use from the Jews was of course his race's only source of hope for survival, tempered by the realisation that the end only needed one bullet.

"With the Germans pulling Jews out of Stutthof and Stuttgart just before liberation by the Allies, were there moments when you despaired of help ever coming?"

"Yes, it was very difficult, as marching back from work to the camp through some villages, civilians could have thrown some bread down, especially earlier in the war. Instead they looked down to see the Jews' wretched conditions, virtually dead people shuffling their feet and skeletons barely alive. And yet these locals would open the windows and spit down at the Jews in total contempt. However, later in the hostilities when the Germans realised that the war was lost, the situation changed again and the windows opened allowing crumbs of bread to flutter down for the beleaguered Jewish prisoners. The consciences of these gentiles had started pricking them, especially as it was becoming evident that the Nazis were losing the battle. The miniscule fragments of dry bread caused bitter struggles between Jews grabbing morsels from the ground, together with more hostility from the guards as progress was delayed in the desperate fighting for the meagre scraps. Those contrasting reactions from the local population were a constant source of despair to the Jewish race. We starving, barely alive prisoners could see no light at the end of the tunnel. We were constantly hoping for the Allies to bomb the SS barracks and at least remove some of those very arrogant, brutal murderers. We were looking for some signs that the world was not indifferent to our suffering in order to give us some glimmer of hope to lift us out from the depths of despair. Nevertheless I was still dreaming, however unrealistically, that one day I shall return to my dear family who I missed so much. This endless longing, this naive hope, I believe, kept me alive from day to day."

The toilet for the war workers was literally a hole in the ground but the Jews by now didn't expect anything else. Reference to the toilet facilities reminded Mayer of a serious question he was asked forty years or more after the war had ended by an exceptionally intelligent man, "did the Germans give you toilet paper?" The Jews saw this 'omission' as not important and would not have seen doing without this facility alone as deprivation.

They were still in Auschwitz clothing and Mayer could see none of the friends he'd met previously, being surrounded totally by strangers. In those years and in those conditions no deep friendships were made because you never knew how long you or your new friend had to live, and losing someone close produced nothing but pain, a commodity that had been in plentiful supply since 1939. Friendships of necessity therefore were usually only superficial.

Although slave labourers were only able to tell the month by the weather, he estimated he was in Gotha until round about the end of March or the very beginning of April 1945, when the Russians were very close and the roads were littered with burning lorries and anti tank weapons ready to attack the Allies.

Chapter Eleven

The death march out of Gotha, undoubtedly the most barbaric and brutal physical test Mayer had ever been asked to undertake, started one evening at 7.30pm when the Jews were made to run along dirt tracks, firstly to avoid the pitiful Jews being liberated by the Allies and secondly because most of the roads were blocked. Some of the inmates, in all probability because a few of the guards were in their forties or even older, tried escaping into the woods, but were closely followed by the German guards spraying the area with machine gun fire. They marched all night and the following day without food or water, although the Germans knocked on doors of houses and were given coffee and cake and various other luxuries. Eventually they were joined by other columns as Europe was being traversed by numerous marches from every direction.

They were taken out and were made to run the first part of that march. They could not use the main roads any more because these were thoroughly clogged with the military and burning lorries and they could see German soldiers were standing there with anti tank weapons. Anyone who could not keep up with the speed of that march was shot on the spot, as were those who felt the need to answer the call of nature. They marched at great speed all night and all day and, after twenty-four hours, they were forced to lay down in an open field with other marchers in adjacent fields. All night they heard shooting and Mayer thought that was to deter the Jews from any thoughts of escape. In the morning the whistle blew to continue the march and many of his colleagues could not get up for they had been shot at random. The final part of that march, over the Thuringian mountains, was more painful than previous because they were tired, hungry and worn out. Heavy rain proceeded to fall and anybody who dropped out to recover, with a view to rejoining the line further back, was shot immediately, one bullet neatly penetrating his head and his body kicked off the road. This continued all the time as stamina expired from skeletal bodies. For the first time in over five years of the most inhuman treatment, Mayer felt total and utter despair and could see no hope whatsoever. It was his lowest point in five years and one month of scheming to survive, taking risks only when his extreme hunger warranted that gamble. He felt he just couldn't take any more and furthermore he knew all he had to do was to stop for a second and a bullet in the back of the head would free his body from pain and torment. He decided to pack it in but, still with a burning desire for freedom, deliberately spoke of his intentions aloud in Yiddish in the faint hope of somebody perhaps helping him to this goal. He could have attracted advice to stop and bite the bullet but two of his neighbours in the line, both total strangers possibly in their late twenties, comforted him and made him reconsider. "You can't give up now, it's five to twelve, the war is almost finished. You've got to fight on and march." The phrase 'it's five to twelve' is a popular phrase in both German and Yiddish and means 'it's almost over'. These complete strangers saved his life, and his dearest wish is that they made it too, although he doubts it since so many were murdered on that journey the conditions were well nigh unbelievable. As the now much smaller group of prisoners passed through Weimar, the capital of Germany prior to Berlin, local civilians were leaving in droves, a sure sign that the Russians were not far away. Merely witnessing German refugees encountering less than one half of one percent of the humiliation that he and others of his kin had suffered for years, gave him a buzz, enabling him to draw on reserves of energy he never knew he had. The sight of disgruntled German civilians pushing their handcarts conveying their worldly possessions looked exactly the same as early in the conflict when all the nationalities under the Nazi jackboot played out similar scenes. It was well nigh impossible to feel sympathy for citizens of the nation that had rewritten the history books relating to man's inhumanity to man.

The march had taken thirty six hours, a day and a half of cruelly fast marching and running inflicted on skeletal Jews more dead than alive, once again with neither food or water. Eventually they arrived at Buchenwald, then being used as a collection centre from all directions, which was already greatly overcrowded by accumulations from surrounding camps. Prisoners slept on the hard cement floor and the miniscule food rations made previous camps look half reasonable. There was no work at Buchenwald, where they spent about a week, clearly able to hear the dull thud of the Allied Artillery in the distance, and yet, still the Germans insisted on inflicting the pain and the futility of roll calls. Morning and night, even at this eleventh hour, numbers mattered to the Third Reich. Accountability of prisoners twice a day deterred many thoughts of escape and, even at this stage of impending defeat, the Germans behaved in a manner that suggested they were still winning the war. Any thoughts that ordinary German soldiers may have had of slipping away to save their skins were snuffed out every time by the presence of the fanatical members of the Waffen SS bringing up the rear of the contingent.

Chapter Twelve

It was April 8th 1945, the Allies were closing in on Buchenwald and it wasn't long before Jews and Russian prisoners of war were taken out and loaded into open coal wagons, one hundred men to a wagon which meant barely standing room if you pack like sardines. This was to be Mayer's most horrendous rail journey of all. Every nightfall their guards, made up of all nationalities, collaborators from Hungary, Ukraine, Latvia and Lithuania, many in their forties and even fifties, were the most sadistic of brutes and in no mood for tolerance. With the butt of their rifle they hit the prisoners over the head and screamed at them to lie down. How could anyone lay when there is even insufficient standing room? But they all had to, because any Jews still standing at the end of the wagon would be shot, a bullet being dispatched unerringly through any head showing over the side of the wagon. The battle that took place there every night was absolutely horrendous. Who was going to lie on whom and how many were going to lie on top of him? Although everyone was incredibly weak by then, it still took quite a few minutes to sort the melee out, much to the pleasure of the watching guards. In the struggle to get air, the strongest would end up on top with the weaker beings suffocating in the lower levels, a mirror image of what the Sonderkommandos would see when first opening the gas chamber doors to reveal the mound of the dead, their struggle for air showing as scratches to faces and other parts of the anatomy. Next morning at least twenty men were dead in each wagon. The pitiful Jews were on this journey for three weeks without food or water, a journey to Theresienstadt that should have taken only two days, were it not for the countless shunting into sidings to allow military trains through. It does pose the question how already grossly weakened people, more dead than alive, can exist for three weeks without food or water, bearing in mind the barbaric nightly fight for life itself with one's colleagues. In fact most of them didn't. Both survivors and their dead colleagues exhibited blood stained arms, legs and faces, souvenirs picked up from daily desperate fighting with bare hands to keep off the bottom of the coal truck. Nails scratched deep into the flesh of former colleagues, every trick in the book was allowed in this very personal battle for survival, where former friendships counted for nought. Every so often the train would be stopped and moved to a siding and people were allowed to get off and the corpses discreetly removed. The survivors managed to collect grass, leaves and snow for water and sit around a fire, whilst both Jews and Russian POWs roasted their shoes over the same fire, hoping to eat the leather from the uppers, so desperate for food were they. Some resorted to cannibalism, especially the Russians, although this was difficult because there was no flesh on the dead bodies and they had to go internally for food. Obviously having no knives on them at that time, they would hack their way into the dead bodies of their former colleagues with whatever they could find, searching probably for the liver. Mayer did not have the heart to do it but in no way did he criticise those who did for the sake of survival.

The Germans took the remaining live Jews, including Mayer, on another train to his ninth camp at Thersienstadt, a ghetto cum camp in Czechoslovakia comprising brick built barracks erected long, long before by the Turks. Just before arriving at the Czech border the Jews were switched to other coal wagons, once again indicating the Nazi zeal in treating Jews like no other race. The transfer was effected quickly and, in the general mayhem existing at that time, at least one Jew hid with the Russians, for Mayer befriended that boy after hostilities had ceased. The abandoned train containing Russian POWs was liberated by Partisans the very next day. He often wondered why the Nazis persisted in moving the Jews yet again but left the Russians to be given freedom. Why spend time and money moving them when, in order to prevent the Allies from talking to the Holocaust victims, all they had to do was to kill the wretches. The whole strategy defied logic.

In April 1945, when Mayer was eighteen and a half years old, his head was completely bald, his hair not growing back at all for a long time, and he weighed barely four stone. Eventually they arrived at Theresienstadt, between seven to ten days before their eventual liberation on May 8th, and here conditions were horrendous with overcrowding on a scale he'd not experienced before. Soon typhus broke out and, since diarrhoea is one of the symptoms of this disease, the toilet was absolutely flooded out with ankle deep excrement. Mayer now had no shirt or vest since he'd used both to clean himself as best he could and of course you can't eat or drink even when food is available. When the Russians came in to liberate the camp, some of his colleagues were fortunate to be free from the infection and they were standing at the window whistling and shouting and singing with great joy on what was a momentous occasion. Mayer was at the point of dying with typhus and was not even able to lift his head, but, nevertheless, that joy filled him with renewed determination to fight the virus and build up his morale in order to continue that most precious of commodities, life itself, for which he had fought so dearly. Not even the elation at his liberation could give Mayer the strength to lift his head up from his bed, so close to death was he, so close that even a delay of twenty-four hours would probably have denied him the chance to continue his life. Liberation was indeed a joyous occasion but, remembering those 1886 days of hard labour, surviving some forty Mengele selections and suffering more than 1500 miles of cattle truck and coal wagon trips, in total lasting about sixty three days with no food or water, it was, without doubt, the most emotional moment of his whole life. He honestly believes that, at that most wonderful moment of liberation, he had less than twenty-four hours to live. The Russians established improvised hospitals and took the former prisoners along to give them a hot shower with soap, a luxury to which he had become unaccustomed for too long. Each patient received a hard-boiled egg, something Mayer had not enjoyed for more than five years. As he was getting a little stronger he noticed his neighbour had quietly passed away, the hard labour and starvation having finally beaten him, a sad sight but one that failed to stop Mayer enjoying the man's untouched egg. Amidst the acute shortages of medicines he remembered fondly the gentle and most compassionate care and understanding afforded to them by a few Russian lady doctors, a most unusual sight in those days.

"What was the thought that went through your head when you took that first bite from an egg for over five years?"

"To me at that time it was an absolute luxury, yet today an egg is something everyone takes for granted. It epitomised survival and freedom and the experience itself was out of this world."

"How did you feel to be free? Can you describe it?"

"I know well the other side, the world of deprivation, humiliation, beatings and abject despair, and so, in answer to your question, there are no words sufficiently powerful to record the degree of my appreciation of freedom. Like so many other blessings in life freedom in more peaceful times is often taken for granted. One of my major regrets was failing to complete my education like children in normal circumstances. I always considered schooling a most wonderful time."

As he was getting stronger and moving around more, Mayer found his old ginger haired friend and realist, Pietruska, motionless in bed with a worse case of typhus even than Mayer's. He immediately noticed Pietruska was leaving his food untouched and Mayer pleaded with him, "you must eat your food, we're free people now and we've been liberated to return to our families." Pietruska replied solemnly, "Mayer, there is no wife and children." He was so extremely distraught on realising he had no wife or children left alive, that Mayer could not prevail on him to pull through and survive. This happy chap, so full of fun normally, who scraped a living together as a shoemaker and shoe repairer, had finally lost his will to live and he passed peacefully away a few days after liberation. Mayer felt his friend could have survived but he had lost the will to live and he was not able to give this vital constituent to him. Many Jews, who had survived the most unimaginable horrors for so many years, died at this, the eleventh hour. Mayer could not save Pietruska and he felt he had let his friend down, for this good man looked after the thirteen year old Mayer on that first cattle truck journey from Sieradz to Otoczno, where he continued to build up the boy's hope and optimism, so vital for any hope of survival. The two friends were at Lusenheim and Guttenbrun together but then didn't meet again until the Russian hospital at Theresienstadt. Mayer felt sad that he hadn't been able to return Pietruska's help when he needed it most. He had tried but failed to change the negative thoughts in his friend's mind into positive ones for the future. For this he was acutely distressed. Pietruska was a realist and he knew for certain that the Germans would never allow a mother and two children to survive, whereas Mayer, clinging to the hope that possibly his elder brother and sister had the same chance as he had, was a little naive which helped him up to a point. Nevertheless the loss of that great friend has often tormented him into wishing it had been Yakov who had been at Theresienstadt for he had been closer to Pietruska and their social ties might just have prevailed on him to save his friend's life.

To survive these dangerous last days of the war a person needed luck on their side for the Germans ideally wanted no Jewish witnesses to tell the outside world of their holocaust. Just before the arrival of Russian troops, the German Commandant at Theresienstadt contacted the Red Cross and told them all Jews were to be exterminated in the German built gas chambers and crematorium in the hills near the camp, but bartered their lives for his family's safe passage. The Red Cross arrived at Theresienstadt two days before the Russians liberated the camp on May 8th 1945, one Nazi Commandant and his family slipped away into the night and, physical health apart, the last barrier to Jewish survival at that camp disappeared. All the German guards left during the evening of the seventh in order to avoid their Soviet counterparts.

"Mayer, would you ever have your Auschwitz number removed?"

"No, why should I?" Mayer retorted with a twinkle in his eye, " this must be a lucky number for me! It is evidence to a happening that some say never happened. This number is testament to the eighteen months that I spent in that Dante's inferno, for no other camp could compare with Auschwitz for crushing Jewish spirits and snuffing out each and every hope of survival. Because this horrific chapter of history must never be forgotten by the generations following, I will take these numbers to the grave."

Recovery saw him released from hospital and returned to the camp from where, with continuing increase in strength, he would walk to the local village where some Jews would encroach on houses abandoned by Germans to look for extra food. Mayer, like a number of his young colleagues, wanted to go to Israel but, whilst still at Theresienstadt, the chance of a new life in Britain presented itself. He was seen by the Jewish refugee committee who announced that they had received special dispensation from the British government for a thousand boys and girls to be sent to the United Kingdom, the only condition being they should be under the age of eighteen. Many of them were over that permitted age, some in their twenties already, because not many people under that age could survive. Soon they were issued with papers to make everyone younger, the twenty year olds becoming seventeen and the eighteen year olds fifteen. Mayer thought how strange life was for in the camps everyone would have to be older than their true age in order to avoid being murdered. Here the opposite applied in order to start a new life and savour freedom.

"Considering your education finished at twelve years of age, how many languages can you speak?"

"Six in total, Polish, Hebrew, Yiddish, German, English and French, the latter being my weakest. German helped save my life and for that I have my mother to thank. As for English, I very soon realised that the English people were not about to learn Polish!" declared the survivor with a sense of humour.

Chapter Thirteen

They could not find a thousand youths for Britain, only a mere seven hundred and thirty two. The final condition was that the Jewish refugee committee was to be totally responsible for their welfare, in other words, they were not to be a burden on the British state. This undertaking was kept to the letter. The first batch of three hundred was to arrive at Carlisle airport on the 14th of August 1945, 290 boys and only ten girls, a clear reflection of the Nazi edict that women of any age were not allowed to survive. From Carlisle they were sent to a most beautiful part of England, Windermere, and there they enjoyed the freedom and the warmth of the local population and those in charge of them as well. By this time Mayer had struck up a good friendship with a lad of similar age to himself, by the name of Ike Alterman who, when the rest of the Jews were transferred to another train bound for Theresienstsdt, had managed to hide and stay with the Russian prisoners of war, being rewarded for his enterprise with liberation the very next day. The two boys had much in common, Ike coming from Sosnowiec, further south in Poland than Sieradz, and he was to marry and settle in Manchester where they brought up two daughters.

They had a locker each and clean sheets, life was truly magnificent. Mayer clearly remembers the first item he ate in Windermere, a trifle, the like of which he has never enjoyed more in all his life. They were looked after by some refugees who came over before the war as part of the kinder transport and these fine people were in charge of both the food and the schooling of the newcomers, Mayer's group being under the watchful eye of Bevish Verna. All there had fared very badly and could not have stayed with people who hadn't suffered as a Jew. The locals were most understanding and even lent their bicycles to the newcomers.

Bread was put on plates and it disappeared immediately, the lads stuffing it in their pockets. This force of habit came about as a direct result of years of deprivation when even pig swill was considered a luxury. Their reaction was not unexpected and they were taken to the kitchens to show them row upon row of loaves that were there today, tomorrow and everyday. They could not believe their good fortune and Mayer's first impression of England was that he had arrived from hell into heaven. Their Hebrew education was restarted and they regularly attended services at the synagogue. Bread was not the only commodity to disappear in those early days in Windermere, for various items of cutlery were also secreted away. Memories of camp experiences, when losing one's soup bowl meant no more soup, were retained and were to fade only very slowly.

From Windermere the Jewish youngsters were split between London, about three hundred of them, Gateshead, Liverpool and the venue to which Mayer was allocated, Manchester. His new city initially was a disappointment to Mayer for it seemed to be permanently besieged by smoke and fog, although he realised immediately how warm in nature were the local people. Rabbi Hans Heineman and his wife to be, Eva Karlbach, both from Germany, were in charge of the hostel in which he stayed. Mayer was keen to practice his English on Beno Penner, a jovial type, who asked in the English exercise, 'would you elope with me?'

He realised that he simply had to catch up on his schooling and, in fact, was given an opportunity of higher education but refused it for the chance of work. Early on in their time in Manchester, the Jews were politely interrogated by the police, on orders from the Home Office. They were asked their own political leanings, as well as those of their parents. Mayer explained that the political aspirations of his parents were essentially nil, their time fully occupied earning a living, following their religion and enjoying family life. Totally non political.

Mayer started work and also took an external Cambridge University degree course, but he soon realised, to keep the two going was impossible and reluctantly he had to give up on education. The Liverpool hostel closed down and their complement joined the Manchester group.

In 1947 a decision was made not to keep the youngsters in hostels too long for fear of them becoming institutionalised. Mayer was sent to the Yochnowitz family, German Jews who came over from their homeland pre war and who lived at 94 George Street. They were a very religious family and obtained a special permission in Germany, as late as 1938 or even 1939, to come over because of the husband's position as a Jewish ritual slaughter man, a specialist job that would not put anyone in England out of work. From there Mayer moved to a bedsit in Seymour Road and started his first job late 1947, early 1948, at a clothing factory in Charlotte Street on a weekly wage of £2.2s. Since his rent was £3 per week, the Jewish Committee made up the difference.

Most of Mayer's experience in the clothing trade, however, was to come later at Naylor's, where he found himself the only Jew on the payroll. Much work was delegated to him and he was given significant freedom with relation to flexible working hours, not to mention excellent tuition. There was a jealous non-Jewish boy in competition with him and he tried to get Mayer fired but failed. Continually trying to provoke Mayer, by talking about Jesus, this totally ignorant young man had his ego dented when told that Jesus was a Jew himself.

From Naylor's in 1951 Mayer took the self-employed route through life. His standards of work were well received by the community but customers found great difficulty spelling his surname and so he contacted the Home Office to ask permission to change his name and whether he needed to go via the deed poll route. The authorities replied in the negative, stating the letter was all that was required, and so, in 1955, Herszkowicz became Hersh. His first passport read, 'Hersh previously known as Herszkowicz'. Every subsequent passport he has received names him simply as Hersh, and so for both practical and sentimental reasons he prizes dearly that first British passport.

The Holocaust had affected Mayer's physical health and he suffered from numerous ulcers. He would wonder if this mass murder could ever happen again and was always sensitive to more modern day ethnic cleansing issues. The effect of his experiences psychologically was more difficult to gauge, although he used to have a great number of nightmares. For numerous years his faith was deeply shaken and he was disillusioned but has since come to realise that Man did this injustice, not God. There are a number of speculative answers on why God allowed these horrendous deeds to be undertaken, some say God looked away, after giving human beings a free will, for good or bad. There were some individuals, albeit not enough of them, who were doing marvellous work in saving human lives. If we had more of them it would be so much better. Communism has failed and he believes democracy is the way to go. Mayer's original plans in his mind involved building up a good business and then going to live in Israel. He believed if Israel had existed pre war many more would have been saved, for other countries in the free world limited the number of Jews they would take. As it was six million Jews perished in the Second World War.

Mayer and his wife-to-be first met on Bury Old Road near Heaton Park in 1951 when his acute shyness was a barrier to a lasting relationship at that time, and besides, his wages certainly could not support two people in those days. Meeting again in the Springfield club on Seymour Road in 1964, the couple continued to see each other, marrying in September 1965.

Coming over to England in 1945 to Mayer was like being born again, a new life free from anti-Semitism. The topic of the war was seldom referred to and nobody English asked the Jews about their experiences, only Jew spoke to Jew about the past. The young Jews had to study and make up for lost time and find and hold down a job as well, for they did not expect the world owed them a living. They didn't want a medal for their experience, for it was nothing to do with Great Britain, only mainland Europe.

"Do you not agree that the free world did not appreciate fully the incredibly extensive scale of the mass murders, otherwise surely they would have taken bombing action against both Auschwitz and the rail network bringing thousands of Hungarian Jews daily to their deaths during 1944? This at a time when the Allies had total air supremacy."

"The world most certainly knew of the atrocities long before they peaked in number in 1944. As early as 1942 Lieutenant Kurt Gerstein, the Berlin based SS officer responsible for the purchasing of Zyklon B, after witnessing its lethal performances at the death camps of Belzec, Treblinka and Sorbibor, realised that he personally could not mentally deal with the matter. On his way back to Berlin by train from Warsaw this Nazi, perspiring heavily from the remembrance of the sights he'd witnessed, engaged in conversation with Baron Von Otter, a Swedish diplomat, to whom he confided the details of the birth of the final solution. Von Otter sent a detailed report of his discussion with Gerstein to his government in Stockholm. Later in the same year Jan Karski, a courier from the Polish underground who had gained first hand knowledge of the camps, reached London with a full report on the status quo relating to the elimination of European Jewry. By the middle of 1944 when the rate of annihilation of Jews reached the dizziest of heights, the Allies had received conclusive proof of the SS atrocities when eye-witness reports from two pairs of escaped prisoners reached London and Washington via Geneva from occupied Slovakia. The accounts of Rudolf Vrba and Alfred Wetzler, both Slovaks, extolled in detail the gassing procedures at Auschwitz, whilst those of Arnost Rosin, a Slovak, and Czeslaw Mordowicz, a Pole, described the arrival and killing of the Hungarian Jews. The shocking news moved Prime Minister Winston Churchill to write to a colleague, *"there is no doubt that this is probably the greatest and most horrible crime ever committed in the whole history of the world"*.

"Your best friend, David Josefowicz, sounded a great character and so brave in his escapades. Can you explain how David coped with the ever burdening memories of the camps as he became older?"

"Firstly David did what most survivors tried to do; to rebuild their lives by working extremely hard. This they did to prove to themselves that they were decent and proud people and to totally reverse the dehumanisation inflicted on the Jewish race by the Fascists. The quality that helped most Jews, David and myself included, was their strong faith in God, whilst in our home life we lived as devout Jews, where we experienced love, sincerity and charity. Quite soon after liberation David started work on a farm in order to gain experience with the ultimate intention of joining a kibbutz in Israel. This mission he did accomplish when reaching Kibbutz Afilium at the Sea of Galilee, being married at that time to a lovely girl called Sara, also a Holocaust survivor. When Israel was attacked by its Arab neighbours in 1948, David fought in the defence of the State. He eventually started work as a builder near Haifa and became a successful entrepreneur. As he aged, his Holocaust experiences appeared to weigh more heavily on him than previously, consequently he retired early and devoted much of his time to Holocaust education. Unfortunately in later life he experienced flashbacks and nightmares in addition to being plagued by ill health. He left Germany to stay with a cousin, by the name of Philipe Jacubouritz in Antwerp, Belgium. Philipe looked after him with great compassion and selfless loyalty but David sadly passed away on the 9th of March 1997, that day, I lost a truly great friend."

Chapter 14

Most Jewish families lost large proportions of both their immediate and extended families. The Herszkowicz family were no exception. About one hundred members of his extended family, aunts, uncles, cousins and second cousins, had lived pre war in Poland, in places like Kalisz, Praszka, Blaszka and Zdunska Wola. Not one survived the Holocaust. His mother's brother, living in Kalisz, was probably exterminated even before January 1941, this area being one of the first to be annexed to the German Reich and made Judenrein, meaning cleansed of Jews. His uncle was taken south to Lublin where he suffered horrific conditions and acute starvation, somehow managing to send a letter to them begging for food and explaining that hundreds of Jews were dying from hunger and disease. They could not accede to this request for they could barely feed their own family and besides there was no way the Germans would pass on food from one Jew to another.

In attempts to find out who, if indeed anyone, of his extended family had survived the Holocaust, Mayer advertised in German newspapers and sent letters to the Red Cross. The latter avenue of search brought rich reward in locating his elder brother, Yakov, who was liberated in January 1945, much earlier than Mayer, and subsequently found himself in a displaced camp in Germany. He made his way to Israel illegally but was caught by the British and put into a camp in Cyprus once again behind barbed wire, by the very people who had liberated so many Jews in the last weeks of the war. Whilst in Cyprus he met a girl called Esther who would eventually become his wife. Yakov never gave up trying to escape and eventually his endeavours brought success when he left Cyprus behind and made good his escape to Israel in a fishing boat. Like so many others after liberation, Yakov's first thought on liberation was to return home to see how many, if any, of his immediate family had survived the traumas of the Holocaust. He firmly believed that other surviving members of his family would likewise seek the solace of their family home. When he knocked on the front door of the pre-war Herszkowicz home it must have been the end of January or even the early days of February 1945. The Polish non-Jewish lady, the new owner, would not let him in. Yakov recognised the furniture of old but had no intention of asking for their accommodation back again, although he decided to stay on a while in Sieradz, until he started to receive threatening notes from Christian Poles, saying that if he wanted to live, it would be advisable for him to get out of Poland. He certainly took this anti- Semitic threat seriously and moved to Germany into a Displaced Person's Camp. What really shocked Yakov and which he found utterly incomprehensible, was that, after all the common suffering and the almost total annihilation of the Polish Jews, how could hatred still exist towards this handful of survivors.

Another person Mayer managed to find through the Red Cross organisation was his uncle, Maurice Herszkowicz, who lived in France both before and after the war. Maurice's mother died in hospital in early 1941. Immediately afterwards the rest of the family were taken and kept for a short time in hay barns until the Germans took them via the gassing vans to Chelmno where their bodies were cremated.

That area of Poland, being so close to the German border, was one of the first to be made Judenrein, cleansed of Jews, around the beginning of 1941.

Maurice left Poland and went to Romilly in France, 130 kms south east of Paris, where he received a warm welcome from the locals and soon became known as the friendly tailor after he opened his shop on Beaulant Giroux Street in 1934. In Eastern Europe the first flashes of the Nazi storm could be seen and, anticipating the forthcoming danger, in 1938 he took on military duty, joining the 94th infantry division at Angouleme.

Although, being a Jew, he had the right to trade taken away from him, he still managed to make ends meet until, one day, he was invited without ceremony by a felgendarm to follow him to the Commandant's headquarters, from where his wife never expected him to return. Fate was to decide matters differently however. To the officer who asked whether he spoke German, Maurice replied in the negative, even though the Gothic language was more familiar to him than that of Moliere was ever to be. Forced to work for the occupiers he overheard their conversations, for the Germans were not wary of this little Jewish tailor whose silence reassured them.

Maurice was contacted by a midwife, a certain Madame Aigle, who revealed to him the existence of a resistance network headed by a railway engineer, Andre Maurice, to whom she introduced him. Maurice Herszkowicz turned out to be a more than useful information agent. He would report what he heard in terms of troop numbers and movements, transfers of superior officers and changes to civilian postings. It was at this time that he became acquainted with a German engineer who had been given responsibility for the air base. No Nazi aircraft took off which was not under his control or without his flight authorisation. A fervent Catholic, this Bavarian was totally against the Nazis and a special relationship was to be born out of the persecution of their two religions. The engineer stressed to Maurice that any information he divulged was not against Germany but would only be levelled as his personal distaste of the Nazi regime. When the Allies needed information on a special kind of Messerschmidt, the German engineer, at the house of Madame Aigle, provided all the sketches detailing the vital parts of the aircraft. The head of the resistance network duly ensured they arrived in the right hands in London.

Maurice was very resourceful in his role as spy-master and, to obtain accurate information on the location of fuel dumps at the airfield, his German engineer friend supplied him with a girl friend, a young lady who worked for the Bavarian collaborator. The sight of two loved ones strolling around the base in their lunch break did not warrant a second glance from the authorities. He would count his footsteps and, from that count, judge as accurately as possible the distance between the fuel dumps and an observable local landmark. Not many nights later Allied bombers scored a direct hit on the target, whilst the time of departure of the German bombers enabled Allied fighters to shoot the enemy planes down before reaching their targets. As a result of the direct hit on the fuel dumps the Germans were watching local workers very closely, Maurice included. He and his wife had two children, the younger of whom, Jaqueline, was difficult to feed because of an eating disorder and was consequently given away to a Christian family. This stroke of great fortune meant she was to survive the Holocaust.

One day his wife, Szprynca, glancing out of the window, screamed "Maurice, the Germans are coming!". As his wife told the intruders that her husband had gone to Paris, he managed to hide behind a door as two guards marched off his wife and eighteen month old baby, Simone, he watched them leave, his heart strangled with anguish. He was saved a second time when the Germans returned to his flat by the prompt response of a neighbour on his landing. He fled to the courtyard, borrowed Monsieur Payen's bike and went to take refuge with Miss Aigle, who hid him for a week. The German engineer re-established contact with Maurice but warned him that he would be unable to continue much longer since those in Nazi circles and amongst the Gestapo were already referring to him as a 'black' or traitor. Consequently this brave German was a condemned man living on borrowed time.

Maurice then went into proper hiding in a village south of that area but he had paid a high price indeed for helping the Allies because both his wife and baby were gassed at Auschwitz. Maurice survived the war and lives today in France.

In order to enable modern generations to truly feel the fears and the worries of the Jewish people, with the constant reference to food and goods and the lack of them, in those dark days of February 1941, a letter from Mayer's aunt Esther to her brother Maurice has been translated from the French and is reproduced here. This letter, dated 20th February 1941, and sent from Krzepice, was one of the last letters to get through from Jew to Jew, for soon afterwards the right of a Jew to send a letter was withdrawn permanently. Nevertheless this correspondence itself would have been heavily censored by the Germans. When the

Germans invaded Russia in June 1941 'postspere' was effected immediately, this meaning simply the stoppage of all post for Jews.

Krzepice, 20th February 1941.

Dear brother and sister in law, Maurice and Szprynca, I have received your postcard for which I thank you with all my heart; I can also write to you to tell that I have received your package yesterday. Believe me my dear, my joy that I've come to express on this piece of paper, is deep. I have cried a lot. I am very happy that you have sent in the parcel a shirt, a dress, a pair of socks and a pair of black tights; this will remain in my mind.

Nacha has also received things from Sahra for herself and the children. We are neighbours, she also does not have anything anymore. Dear brother, I thank you for the parcel that you have sent to my dear husband. This week I have received a letter from him in which he asks me for some bread; once again, my dear brother, I thank you for everything.

Now dear, I am writing to you about my dear mother. She got a bad cold in the barn and her heart is still weak. First of all we were at Szlama and afterwards in the countryside. She told me that she would never return to Praska, but I begged my mother not to speak like that and not to cry, because everything would be for the best and I called the doctor everyday. Afterwards, I made her go to hospital. Unfortunately she did not stay there long. I have very often visited her and brought her some food. As soon as she saw me, she was the happiest person on Earth, each time she said to me, "Esther my dear child, do not cry and keep the food for yourself, you will see it will get better".

That is how she spoke to me on Saturday and she begged me to reunite all the children, she always called Maurice, Paola, Loja, Szlamek and my brother in law helped me to carry her to the hospital on Saturday and on Sunday I went to see her. As soon as she heard my voice, she sat down and to please me, she ate the apples and the other things that I had brought her.

I stayed with her but she begged me to bring little Jacques whom she wanted to see. Until the last minute she was conscious. And then on Monday morning at 6 am, the sister came to wake me up to announce to me the death of our dear Mum. She was 65 years old. I ran to the hospital, she was in the mortuary.

Dearest, what strength I need to write all of that. She changed so much that she was unrecognisable. I prayed for you all. I have been several times to her tomb.

Szlamek was also at the funeral as well as some inhabitants of Praszka. My dear brother, do you know the address of our brother, Levy, in order to write to him about it? She has been dead for eight days. I feel ill with crying. All my thoughts go to our dear mother. Remember that she died on the 8th.

I salute you and I kiss you and so does my son Jacques. My dearest, do not forget to write to us. My sister Paola has sent a few things for my son. I will send you some pictures of him.

I kiss you with all my heart, your sister, Esther and Jacques.

Write back straight away. Best wishes to my sister in law and your dear child.

Your sister,
Esther.

Maurice also had an elder brother, Mordcha, who lived in Paris and was also in the French army but unfortunately he died in action in 1940 and is buried in a French cemetery. Mordcha's wife, Helen, and their three children were in hiding and were picked up in the street by Partisans and given shelter, enabling all four to survive the war. Two of the children, cousins Charles and Rosette, died naturally in the fifties and later Helen and her son, Jacques Hersh, emigrated to America where he served his national service before returning to Europe. Aunt Helen lived to the ripe old age of ninety four whilst Jacques and his wife Ellen are prolific and successful authors and live today in Copenhagen.

Mayer's brother in law to be, Arnold Kupfer, left Europe for Montevideo in Uruguay, sadly without his fiancée, Mayer's dear sister, Kajla. Once he heard that Kajla had perished, he eventually married in Uruguay before subsequently emigrating to Israel and setting up home at Haifa, where Mayer had the pleasure of visiting. Mayer advertised in German newspapers printed in North America, the main one being 'Aufbau', meaning in English, 'rebuilding', and it was through this newspaper during 1947/48 that he found Arnold in Montevideo, Uruguay.

David Josefowicz, always the risk taker, was one of Mayer's closest friends, going back to their school days when they did their homework together and they were together at that first labour camp of Otoczno. David was almost a year younger than Mayer and, when he first arrived at Auschwitz, had some good fortune in that he was billeted to a barrack containing some non-Jewish Poles from his home town of Sieradz, ensuring him of some convivial conversation as well as some help with food.

Because he looked very young, David was subsequently put into the kinder block which he soon realised was a take off point for the gas chambers. Sure enough shortly afterwards, in the middle of the night, the youthful contents of the kinder block were herded away en route to their elimination point. In the melee he escaped to the latrine and eventually to his father's acquaintance, the friendly block leader. David's good fortune didn't end there for later on in that infamous death camp, some non-Jewish Poles who had the good fortune to receive Red Cross parcels, kindly shared their bounty with the young Jew from Sieradz.

The two school chums parted company after Auschwitz, David being liberated much earlier than Mayer in East Prussia and, from January to May 1945, joined the Russian army to push the Nazis back into Germany. Imagine his joy at fighting the Germans on their own soil and, in particular, entering Berlin with the triumphant Red army. At that moment his sense of fulfilment in witnessing the last throes of the Third Reich, after all the atrocities and humiliations he'd experienced, must have been immense.

David was well versed in the formation of a Jewish group, intent on judgement and vengeance against high-ranking Nazis on the run all over Europe at the end of hostilities. All Jews shared a common desire when peace finally arrived, to get out, to get out of the camps, and to get out of the accursed continent of Europe. Jewish communities had existed in Europe for over two thousand years and, in that time, of the one hundred generations of Jew, not one had been spared the painful burden of paying tribute in blood to the non-Jewish majority. In the Second World War no single race suffered as horrendously as the Jew, their loss in proportion to population being six times greater than

Russia's, eight times greater than Poland's, ninety times greater than England's and five hundred times that of the Americans. These spirited Jews, thirsting for retribution against the major players of the evil Nazi regime, formed themselves into an organisation known as DIN, a Hebrew word meaning judgement, and from 1945 have taken vengeance, and imposed the judgement of the Jew, upon those who killed Jews. David told Mayer that their successes included the execution of SS Brigadier General Dr. Wilhelm Albert, Chief of the Security Police at Lodz. He was awarded the SS Ehrendegun (Dagger of Honour) for his role in the final liquidation of the Lodz ghetto, August-September 1944. Another highly desirable elimination and close to many Jewish hearts, was SS Major Hans Bothmann, commander of the 'Bothmann Sonderkommando' which supervised the Chelmno gas chambers 1942-44, except for April 1943, when he was transferred as an 'expert' to the SS Prince Eugen Division for the second Lodz ghetto massacre. A third Jewish trophy, even closer to home for the two school chums from Sieradz, was Mr. Bleim, Chief SS Commandant in the ghetto of their own hometown. His finding took an incredible amount of work over many years and only went to show the great tenacity of the DIN organisation. Bleim, who gave orders for cruel torture and sadistic killing to many inhabitants of the ghetto of Sieradz, was eventually tracked down to a bungalow in Bucholt, Germany. Bleim by then had a son in Canada but one night in 1983 his residence was mysteriously burnt to the ground with both him and his wife inside. Thus, thirty-eight years after cessation of the fighting, vengeance was exacted on a perpetrator of evil, a Nazi who no doubt thought he was beyond retribution but forgot that tormented Jews have long memories.

"What are your feelings toward the Germans now, Mayer?"

"Strange as it may seem to you, I do not feel any hatred toward Germany. That, however, is not to say I admire those people who took part in these most terrible and hideous murders, for they did that out of hatred. They imbued with prejudice racial hatred and that gave them the justification to murder all those millions of innocent people. I would not lower myself to their level in having hatred in my heart, because to me, hatred was the main cause of the Holocaust. For them I have nothing but contempt. Of course I cannot aim these remarks at Germans alone, for there were many collaborators of numerous nationalities active in this despicable process. Murdering volunteers came from many of the occupied European countries, for example Slovakia, Austria, Poland, Ukraine, Hungary, Lithuania and Latvia to mention but a few. These willing collaborators carried out mass exterminations with great zeal and brutality."

In 1961 a very fit David came over to Britain by boat, bringing with him his car, a small Fiat, and by then he was a very successful builder. Their memories were shared again but, although relatively affluent, because of a far from happy second marriage, he didn't seem as contented as previously, although Mayer remembered how utterly taken he was with Bournemouth. Around 1975 David returned to live in Europe, to Stuttgart in Germany and later, especially toward the end of the seventies, David did much work on Polish television who wanted to show how brutal was Nazism and how Communism was always in the forefront of fighting the swastika and all it stood for. In the early eighties David started suffering from minor strokes but, in 1983, experienced a stroke of major proportions. He discharged himself from hospital and drove to Poland. Minor strokes continued to plague him. In the early nineties, when in a Swiss hospital, his money ran out and he eventually resided in an old folk's home in Germany but he escaped, one time when his training in the camps stood him in good stead. Mayer suggested he go and stay with his cousin in Antwerp, this he did and this relation looked after him well. In his later years, this dear school pal and best friend, was broken both mentally and physically, finally passing away in 1997.

Mayer was so distraught at his pal's death, nearly a year the younger of the two, David was so brave throughout the war, riding his luck at times, but nevertheless showed outstanding courage in some frightening situations. His mind went back to David knocking on the door of a house en route from the rail head back to Otoczno pleading for food, collaborators reported him, resulting in a vicious beating. He avoided hanging because he was less than fourteen years old. Shortly afterwards he escaped back to Sieradz but was recognised by a local policeman, beaten again and returned to Otoczno. Bound for the gas chambers in Auschwitz, he escaped from the kinder block and hid up to his neck in human excrement. At great personal risk, he smuggled explosives to the Sonderkommandos for their famous resistance to tyranny and, on liberation, joined the Red Army and went all the way to Berlin with them. Mayer was so proud of his best friend, one incredibly brave man.

The two school chums searched for each other after the hostilities ceased, eventually making contact in the late forties, his first meeting with David falling around 1953-

54 in Motzkin near Haifa. David had met his girlfriend, Sara, whilst in an internment camp in Cyprus and the two were happily married. Always the hardest of workers, he had developed into a builder of some esteem and was very successful. Both survivors reminisced over past times, both happy and traumatised, for the two pals were experiencing nightmares. David was happily contented with his life but could be quite serious, and by this time, had developed a somewhat sardonic sense of humour. During that two week visit to Israel, when Mayer also met his brother, Yakov, and his sister's former fiancé, Arnold Kupfer, he realised conditions in Israel were particularly tough with many material shortages. David had remarried but the second marriage was not a particularly happy one. He cut a sad sight for he had no children. They met up again in the eighties when David had returned to Europe, living just outside Stuttgart. They planned on visiting Poland to see their birthplace, which promised to be a traumatic experience and was a trip that Mayer wanted, and yet didn't want, to make. In October 1987 they left Stuttgart by car bound for Sieradz where they stayed in a non-Jew's house, a good post war friend of David's. They visited the ghettos in Warsaw, Lodz and Sieradz and also took in Kalisz, where Mayer's mother was born. Mayer did not want to go to Auschwitz but they did go to Chelmno, the final resting place for his mother and three younger brothers. All there is at Chelmno now is a monument to the nigh on 400,000 killed there and also in a clearing in the forest numerous ravines where bodies had been buried. Most victims of Chelmno were cremated and their ashes thrown into the River Ner to hide the evidence of mass murder. Chelmno-on-Ner was near Lodz and the organising of the mass

extermination camp there was begun in November 1941, it being active from December 8th 1941 to January 1945. The victims were mainly Jews from the provinces of Lodz and Poznan and children from the Zamosc district and the Czech village of Lidice. The bodies were cremated in the Rzuchow forests, near the road connecting Kolo with Dabie.

"How would you say your mental state was affected by the experiences you went through?"

"There is no doubt that my mental state was very fundamentally affected by the experiences in the camps, the scars were there, not only from my own physical suffering, but also from losing the rest of my family at a very early age in such a horrible way. This pain is so great that I cannot possibly get it out of my mind and I cannot accept it. A question I am always asking myself is "why? why? why?. There have been no answers yet and this is very painful to me. I cannot really reconcile it for, no matter how much I know about human nature, and I am still learning about it now, this quality can be so cruel, cynical and hateful, not only to kill my family but also some individuals can deny the Holocaust ever happened. We must remember the deaths of all our dear families at the hands of the Nazis and their collaborators for, that is all we can do and not remembering them is akin to murdering them twice. Our enemies would like us to forget all about our innocent families who were murdered at such a relatively young age, but we have a duty to remember them because, not to do so, would be the cruellest cut imaginable. Also we must remember the perpetrators because, if we don't, we should only encourage similar tragedies to befall any race."

There was a local non-Jewish Pole crying vehemently in remembrance of his Jewish girl friend who, after she had been taken away, was killed there with the multitudes of others. After recovering his composure, this Pole took them to see a male friend of his who, during the war, was a forester and an eye witness to what went on there. His account was gruesome in its simplicity because, as a forester, he was supplied with a good pair of binoculars, and was obviously allowed to use them constantly, and saw a myriad of miseries. Thousands arrived daily with none leaving, not a single one, just smoke issuing forth. Many were taken to a church in Kolo where they undressed and were forced into gassing vans.

On arrival in Sieradz the statistics they gleaned from the authorities were frighteningly simple and simply frightening. Out of the five thousand Jews in pre war Sieradz only fifty returned in 1945. Because they had little if any family left, forty eight of them went to Russia and the remaining two had since died. The stark fact of the matter on that October day in 1987 was that there was not a single Jew living in Sieradz. The two ex school chums met two old non-Jewish Poles, aged around seventy, and their single retort was, "Oh, you've survived". There was resentment in their voices that came across loud and clear. It was a most horrible moment to have to endure, David nudged Mayer indicating it was time to leave. The block of flats where Mayer lived had been demolished ten years earlier and, as they left, it would be fair to say that neither had many happy memories of the Polish people.

After visiting Chelmno, Mayer couldn't sleep and took a long time to recover; his wife had told him she thought he should not go and he knew after the event that she was most certainly right. He has often been asked if he could forgive the Germans for what they did. He could never forgive the crimes involved in killing his innocent family, extended family, schoolmates, in fact, his whole community. Besides, how can he forgive the Germans when his family are not here to agree with him. Not one single German has asked him to forgive them. Many of the perpetrators of these evil acts are still alive today and these he despises.

"What was the downside of your return to Poland?"

"Even though there was not one Jew then living in my hometown, Sieradz, the undisguised hostility to my race from old men, who remembered the pre-war Jewish presence, was so extremely disturbing that it made my dear friend, David, want to leave instantly. It was a particularly shattering experience when you consider that the Polish Jews contributed immeasurably to that country's economy, they served in the army and equally sacrificed their lives in the defence of Poland. Not only were all our assets taken away by our fellow Christian Poles, which we did not even attempt to claim back, but, when war ended and so precious few Jews returned, they were made so incredibly unwelcome. Knowing my mother and three younger brothers perished there and realising its great significance in respect of total numbers murdered, made Chelmno a hideously distressing place to visit."

"I don't suppose you have a good story about the Nazis, have you Mayer?"

"That is an excellent question, my friend, and I am going to surprise you by telling you that I do have such an account. In April in either 1998 or 1999, a Danish Jew and Member of Parliament addressed a meeting in Manchester to commemorate the ghetto uprising in Warsaw and included a fascinating true account about the wartime experiences of some of Denmark's Jewish population. As a result of the Danish-German Agreement of the 9th of April 1940, when the Germans occupied Denmark, they embarked on a policy of co-operation and negotiation with the Danish authorities. Consequently the Jews had been unmolested. In August 1943 as Danish resistance stiffened against the German occupation, the Third Reich abolished the Agreement and declared martial law. The SS recognised this as an opportunity to deport all of Denmark's 7,200 Jews but the Supreme German Commander, receiving an order to round up all Danish Jews, for reasons known only to himself, leaked this information to some politically important Danes, giving them precious time to rescue most of that race by ferrying them in boats to neutral Sweden. Only five hundred Jews remained, either because they could not reach the boats in the time allowed, or they were reluctant to leave Denmark. This group were rounded up by the Nazis and taken on the 1st of October 1943 to Theresienstadt. The Danish Red Cross insisted that these Danish Jews, considered equal citizens, should be treated fairly but, since this international organisation had previous experience of how hollow German promises could be, the Danes requested German permission to visit their countrymen in Theresienstadt. Not wanting to particularly flout the International body, the Germans used delaying tactics in order to enable them to falsify the situation. The visitors were shown Jews in suits sitting outside cafes smoking and having coffee whilst other prisoners were walking free and working in factories under reasonable conditions. Two football teams played a match to further emphasise the reasonable normality of the conditions under which the Danish Jews lived. The Germans were very clever in this art of deception, even though the Danes had to be receiving better food rations than their brothers across the rest of Europe. The brilliant sham lasted but a day and, as soon as the Danish Red Cross members left, the facade was pulled down and the prisoners put back to their usual routine. For the two football teams this grandiose occasion would not be repeated, their lifelong aspirations on the field would never be fulfilled. Those sporting prisoners in their entirety were sent to Auschwitz for extermination. Nevertheless, at the end of hostilities, four hundred and twenty three Danish Jews returned to their homes in Scandinavia, an amazing story of the Germans keeping their word, the instance best described as 'one against the wind'."

His voice gradually petered out and there was a distinct pause while the endless seconds, it seemed, ticked away. An exhausted Mayer Hersh eventually broke the silence, "That's it, that's my story, at least all I can remember of it." I was quick to respond, "Your talk has had a tremendously galvanising effect on me, simply to be in the presence of someone who was actually there, someone who witnessed so many of the indescribable horrors. Enlightening members of today's and tomorrow's generations will be important for the memory of your family and friends who perished in the mass murders, and particularly for Pietruska, who lived to be liberated but died shortly afterwards. For this close friend, who had always looked out for you during the darkest of days, it was most important that people should never be allowed to forget."

Chapter 15

"What are the reasons why Jews seem so hated, Mayer?"

"This hatred comes, in the main, from anti-Semitism preached by the church for many centuries, supported by the intelligentsia with the ignorant masses blindly following without question. For many ulterior motives this hatred continued for numerous centuries. Anti-Semites would create blood libels in order to form pogroms, a Russian word meaning the gathering together and killing of Jews. In a blood libel, some Christians would kidnap two Jewish boys, hiding them or sometimes killing them. Anti-Semitism, certainly in Poland, varied in intensity according to the time of year. At Christmas when Jesus was born Christians would not show their anger so much because they were happy about his birth. At Easter, on the other hand, Catholics would be irate at the Jews for repeating the old re-hashed lie that the Jews killed Jesus Christ and anti-Semitic actions would escalate, despite it being a known historical fact that the Romans crucified him. An old story I first heard many years ago might throw some light on this antagonism between Jew and Gentile. 'A Jewish boy was attacked by a Christian boy and he said, "why are you hitting me?". The Christian replied, "because you killed our Christ. The Jewish boy responded, "Wait a minute, firstly Jesus died two thousand years ago and secondly, the Romans killed him." So the Christian boy countered, "I've only just heard about it". It's an old story but one that perhaps helps to put things in perspective.

This hatred dates back many centuries, particularly to the notorious Crusades, which were sanctioned by the Pope in the eleventh to thirteenth centuries. As the Crusaders were travelling through Europe, they were attacking and murdering Jewish communities. One of their aims was to convert the Jews to Christianity, yet the victims were hardly given a choice. Later, in the fifteenth century, the Spanish Inquisition occurred when the Jews were murdered, forcibly converted to Catholicism or expelled. This persecution of the Jewish minorities persisted without any respite right throughout Europe. This totally unjustified hatred toward the Jews had no logic to it. It was nothing less than prejudice, envy and bigotry and would lead to Jews being made the scapegoats by any country experiencing economic or political problems."

"I know the world has seen ethnic cleansing in Yugoslavia and Africa amongst others since the Second World War, but do you honestly feel there is even a remote possibility that the Holocaust could be repeated?"

"Without doubt I believe the Holocaust could well be repeated at some time in the future, mainly because of two reasons, firstly the growth of neo-Nazi movements across Europe and secondly the ignorance existing about the very fact that the Holocaust occurred. There was a Swedish survey on the subject held in 1997, the report of which was published in 1998. The then Swedish Prime Minister, Goeran Persson, called for increased efforts to stop the rise of these neo-Nazi groups throughout Europe. He urged cooperation in information and training to spread knowledge about the Holocaust. The survey showed over ten percent of school children in Sweden did not even know what the Holocaust was. The premier stressed increasing awareness within schools together with stopping the growth of these Nazi movements, otherwise this unspeakable evil could take the stage again. A very recent poll of questions appertaining to the Second World War, and held in Germany, showed that a large number of Germans are sick of being confronted with the Nazi past, and sixty percent feel neither guilty nor responsible for the Holocaust. With Germany worried about rising neo-Nazism, the survey showed that the nation was less and less ready to be a prisoner of its past. Fifty three percent of Germans refuse to agree that there is 'no excuse' for the Holocaust, saying instead that the Germans should be forgiven for crimes committed by their forebears under Hitler. Giving credence to concern by educators and politicians, the poll also found fifty seven percent believe that young Germans learn too little about the Nazi era in school. Since the opening of the Berlin Wall in 1989 and the reunification of Germany in 1990, there has been waves of nazi violence, anti-Semitism, fascism and German nationalism have all spread successfully, and the secret network of ex-Waffen SS men have been shown to be the power behind the international neo-Nazi scene. Fascist terror has also disturbed peaceful everyday life in Britain, Sweden, Norway, the USA and Canada. Since 1989, nationalism in Germany has grown at a terrifying pace and has been accompanied by a level of political violence from the extreme Right, not seen since the days of the Weimar Republic when Hitler's fascists sought to terrorise all opposition. This violence, which has resulted in more than 80 fascist killings since 1990 and more than 23,000 Right-wing extremist crimes investigated by the German police in 1993 alone. Since reunification, Germany has been the recipient of numerous protests and complaints about racism, anti-Semitism and fascism from the USA, Russia, Poland, Denmark, Czechoslovakia, Nigeria, Portuguese and Israeli governments, the United Nations refugee organisation UNHCR, the World Jewish Congress, Amnesty International and the US human rights organisation Helsinki Watch.

In Germany there exists the Fascist Deutsche Volksunion (DVU), the Nazi Nationaldemokratische Partei Deutschlands (NPD), whilst a rival Fascist organisation is Republikaner Partei.

In France, the Front National's Department Protection Securitie (DPS) preach an ideology that is racist and particularly anti-Semitic.

The British National Party (BNP) has neo-Nazi feelings running high, whilst its offshoot, 'The American Friends of the BNP' has raised thousands of dollars in meetings across the USA and through the publication of its newsletter, 'Heritage and Destiny'. In doing so, it is flouting a law that was designed to prevent US Nazis raising funds for Hitler, this being the 'Foreign Agents Registration Act of 1938'.

On Saturday 17th April 1999 a nail bomb exploded in Brixton, South London, injuring fifty people. Two British Nazi groups, Combat 18 and the White Wolves, claimed responsibility. Less than a week after the bombing, a statement was issued by the 'Command Council of The White Wolves'. In a letter sent to news outlets and magazines the group announced, 'Notice is hereby given that all non whites and Jews, the latter defined by blood, not religion, must permanently leave the British Isles before the year is out.

In Austria, Jorg Haider's Freedom Party has distinct neo-Nazi leanings, emanating without doubt from its Austrian leader. His father, Robert Haider, joined the Hitler Youth movement in 1929 and later the SA. He fled to Nazi Germany in 1933, joined the German army, and in July 1934 took part in the Nazi uprising in Austria. His mother, Dorothea, held leading posts in the Hitler Youth for girls (BdM). Jorg's timetable of events and personal quotations had a familiar ring to it, echoing those disturbing rumbles of the thirties.

1987 Jorg held secret meeting with Norbert Burger, a leading Nazi activist.

1990 He appreciated the engagement of the Waffen SS and the Deutsche Wehrmacht in World War 2 as 'a struggle for freedom and democracy'.

Years later, at a time before he was hanged in Israel, Adolf Eichmann wrote the final summation of the long, long record. 'The plain fact was,' said the orchestrator of the final solution truthfully, 'that there was no place on earth that would have been ready to accept the Jews.'

During the latter part of 1944, Britain also obstructed an American plan to trade German expatriates for thousands of Jews dying in concentration camps across Europe, partly because Anthony Eden, the Foreign Secretary, feared they would flood Palestine. Eden believed the humanitarian plan was impractical and conflicted with Britain's policy of limiting Jewish immigration into Palestine, then a British mandate.

I believe this absorbing account revealed a side to Mayer Hersh of which I was already aware, one of, if anything, understatement and total absence of exaggeration. This simplistic and sober approach, so devoid of dramatisation, made the context all the more riveting. I was already aware of his tattooed numerals and their Holocaust implications but, after hearing the details of his five years two months of hard labour in no less than nine labour camps and extermination centres, I was beginning to appreciate why this man is so very special. One fact, which is particularly amazing, is totting up the downside of his years of suffering, starting with a destroyed childhood. I find it hard to take in just how much he lost during those dark years, his family, his home, his community. Only he and his elder brother, Yakov, survived of his immediate family whilst from the one hundred members of his extended family living pre-war in that western part of Poland, not one single person drew breath after hostilities ceased in 1945. Notwithstanding this enormous degree of pain and emotional distress, he tells his story without bitterness, without rancour, without hatred because, in a wonderful way, and quite literally, his humanity has triumphed over all the evil he has witnessed and suffered. Without doubt, that makes Mayer a very special and a very precious individual, and my opportunity of hearing his account a rare and exceedingly memorable privilege.

. The important and over riding lesson emanating from Mayer's story is that future generations should not be allowed to forget the incredible privations suffered by the Jewish race at the hands of the Nazis. Why should the world not be told about the humiliation, the degradation, the inhumane conditions, the starvation, the total absence of hygiene and the wanton brutality. Jews who bore witness to the fact should speak out about the sadistic beatings, the fact that Jews were not permitted a sound night's sleep due to incessantly speeding up roll calls and the general inhumanities served up every minute of every day. Guards beating a prisoner to death were looked upon favourably by the Nazi hierarchy, for a Jewish life was not viewed as being worth the cost of a bullet. Holocaust survivors are a dying breed, the day will come in the not too distant future when nobody will be present to tell the goings on in those infamous camps. Younger generations together with those following must pass the message about the mass murders of an innocent race down the line, for to be constantly aware might just be sufficient to prevent a re-run of the horrors.